CRESSIDA BLYTHEWOOD

How To Escape The Duke And Catch His Brother

This book was professionally typeset on Reedsy.
Find out more at reedsy.com

Contents

1

A Lady's Practical Guide to Escaping a Duke and Pursuing His Brother

As recorded by Lady Araminta Wexley (soon to be something else entirely)

- **Step One: Get Engaged to the Wrong Brother.**

Ideally, this should be done in a public library, a drawing room, or any location sufficiently respectable to disguise the absolute lunacy of the situation. Bonus points if the duke in question is handsome, wealthy, and as emotionally expressive as a tea tray. That way, when he proposes, you'll barely register it happened—until there's a diamond on your finger and an announcement in The Morning Gazette.

- **Step Two: Ignore All Instincts.**

You will have them—those pesky things called instincts. They will whisper things like, "This man has the emotional warmth of a snowbank" or "Why does his younger brother keep smiling at me like we share an inside joke when we've barely spoken?"

Ignore these. Smile politely. Sit through endless dinners. Try not to throw your napkin at anyone.

- **Step Three: Attend One (1) Masquerade.**

Lose your head. Lose your senses. Possibly lose your reputation in the hedge maze behind the orangery. Accidentally kiss the wrong Greycourt. (Or the right one, depending on whom you ask.) Discover that desire is not always sensible—and that it sometimes has very good cheekbones.

- **Step Four: Flee London Immediately.**

When scandal looms like a very persistent goose, remove yourself to the countryside. Choose a remote location, ideally one with at least two opinionated aunts, a poor selection of eligible bachelors, and absolutely no Greycourts.

- **Step Five: Do Not Read the Letters.**

He will write. Do not read them. Especially not aloud. Especially not while lying dramatically across a chaise lounge, whispering his name to the ceiling like a lunatic heroine in a Gothic novel.

(No, you are not in love. You are simply... curious. In a highly emotional, borderline reckless way.)

- **Step Six: If He Arrives—Run Again.**

Unless he brought cake. Or flowers. Or the ability to apologize using fewer metaphors than a Shakespearean actor on his third sherry. In which case... perhaps hear him out. But with your arms crossed and one eyebrow raised. Dignity must be maintained. Even when your heart is thundering like a cavalry charge.

- **Step Seven: Whatever You Do, Don't Marry Him.**

Unless, of course, you want to.

In which case—do.

And invite the duke. He may even smile this time.ß

2

Bound by Duty

Araminta

Thaddeus Greycourt, the Duke of Renshawe, had all the romantic charm of a tax audit, and today was the day my family's accounts were being ruthlessly settled. He slid a diamond ring onto my finger as though he were sealing a business deal, which, of course, is precisely what he was doing.

I sat still in my father's library, a practiced smile affixed to my face while my stomach did a most unladylike churn. Outside, carriages clattered by as if the world remained stubbornly unchanged. Inside, my life was being signed away for the price of a title and a cleared ledger.

The Duke said nothing. He adjusted his cuffs and stared just above my left shoulder, as if he'd found a fascinating flaw in the wallpaper. I had the distinct impression that I was a contractual clause he'd rather not read too closely.

The library had once been my sanctuary—ink-scented, sunlit, a haven from London's chaos. Now it felt like a tomb awaiting its newest occupant. Dust motes floated like gilded ghosts in the golden light. My hands lay in my lap, fingers twisting beneath the silk, the only part of me that dared to betray my panic.

To my left, Papa paced nervously. The sound of his boots against the polished wooden floor echoed like the frantic heartbeat of a man who understood his daughter's future was the final, desperate wager on the table.

"Lady Araminta," the Duke began at last, his clipped baritone slicing through the silence, "I trust your father has explained *our situation* clearly."

Our situation, I thought wryly. *As if we were shipwrecked on a desert island together, rather than him being the ship and I the cargo.* I nodded slowly, forcing my voice to remain steady. "Yes, Your Grace. Papa has been quite clear."

The Duke inclined his head a fraction of an inch, an acknowledgement that betrayed no emotion whatsoever. "Very good. Then you understand that the marriage between us is necessary and beneficial for both families. Your father's debts will be cleared, and you shall gain the stability of a duchess's position."

Stability. A fine word for a gilded cage. I lifted my chin, trying to mirror his cool detachment. "I understand, Your Grace."

Papa halted abruptly, his red-rimmed eyes pleading. "Your Grace, I cannot thank you enough for your generosity. You have saved our family from ruin."

Thaddeus Greycourt lifted a gloved hand, dismissing the gratitude as one might wave away a bothersome insect. "No thanks are necessary, Lord Wexley. It is merely a sensible arrangement."

A sensible arrangement. I had to physically restrain myself from flinching. A public hanging was also a sensible arrangement for dealing with a criminal, I supposed. Efficient, final, and entirely devoid of pleasantry. I studied the Duke, searching for any hint of softness. His features were undeniably handsome, a classical sculpture of a man, but his coolness was a chilling varnish that erased any potential warmth.

"If there is nothing else, perhaps we should proceed with the formalities," the Duke suggested, his tone perfectly indifferent.

Papa's hands trembled as he retrieved a small velvet box from his desk. He handed it to the Duke with a strained smile, his eyes meeting mine in a silent apology for the sacrifice he required.

The Duke rose, his every movement precise. He crossed the short distance to stand before me, towering over my seated form. My heart hammered against my ribs, a frantic bird trapped in a cage of bone. With careful precision, he

5

opened the box. The ring glinted within, a circle of diamonds that seemed to absorb all the light in the room and reflect none of the warmth.

My hand trembled slightly as I offered it to him. He took my fingers, his grip surprisingly gentle yet so devoid of heat it was almost clinical. It was the touch of a physician checking for a pulse before pronouncing the patient dead. He slid the ring onto my finger, his gaze still resolutely fixed on the wall behind me.

"With this ring, our arrangement is sealed," he pronounced calmly. "We shall announce our engagement formally at Lady Millicent's ball tomorrow evening."

"Of course, Your Grace," I murmured.

He stepped back, released my hand, and resumed his seat as though the moment had been nothing more than signing a receipt. Papa visibly sagged with relief. "Splendid. Absolutely splendid. You honor us, Your Grace."

The Duke's lips twitched, a gesture so fleeting it was less a smile and more a muscular spasm. "Then, if there is nothing further, I will take my leave. My secretary will see to the necessary announcements."

He stood, nodded curtly to my father, and then inclined his head briefly toward me. "Lady Araminta." He said my name as if reading it from an inventory list.

One Lady Araminta, acquired.

"Your Grace," I replied softly, my throat tight.

When the door closed behind him, Papa sank heavily into a chair, burying his face in his hands. "Forgive me, Araminta. I never wanted this for you."

I rose, crossing the room to kneel beside him. "Papa, please don't. You did what was necessary."

He shook his head miserably. "You deserve better. You deserve love, not a cold transaction."

"I deserve to protect my family," I corrected gently. "If this is the price, then it's one I must pay."

Papa lifted his head, his eyes full of remorse. "He will not make you happy, Araminta."

I forced a smile that felt brittle enough to shatter. "Happiness can be found in many places, Papa. Perhaps it simply requires a more thorough search when one is a duchess."

Even as I spoke, I doubted it. Could warmth ever bloom from such icy ground?

"You've always been brave, my dear girl," Papa murmured, patting my hand. "I pray that your courage does not fail you now."

I stood, smoothing my gown. Courage had always been my refuge, duty my shield. Perhaps they could protect my heart from breaking entirely. "I shall manage, Papa," I assured him, more to myself than to him. "We Wexleys are made of stronger stuff than heartbreak."

Or perhaps, I thought, as I stepped into the hallway, *we are merely better at hiding the cracks.* The Duke's ring felt impossibly heavy on my finger, a beautiful, brilliant manacle. It seemed duty had finally caught up with me, and I had never felt more trapped.

3

Frigid Formalities

Araminta

My engagement to the Duke of Renshawe had begun. This meant my life was now an endless series of polite performances. The first of these was an afternoon tea at the home of my mother's dearest friend, Lady Vexhall. The name, I had always thought, was entirely too appropriate.

Lady Vexhall's drawing room was a masterpiece of suffocating opulence. Everything was gilded. The chairs were gilded. The mirror frames were gilded. Even the small, nervous-looking cherubs painted on the ceiling seemed to have been dusted with gold leaf. It was the sort of room designed to announce its owner's wealth so loudly that one could scarcely hear oneself think. Perhaps that was the point.

I sat on a chintz sofa that was far too soft, sinking into it as if the house itself were trying to consume me. To my right sat the Duke. His presence was a tangible thing, a block of cold, silent judgment in an otherwise overheated room. He did not sink. He sat perfectly, his posture an affront to the sofa's plush intentions. He made the furniture look servile.

To my left, my mother, Beatrice Wexley, was practically vibrating with social triumph. She wore her finest afternoon gown of periwinkle blue, her smile stretched so wide I feared her face might crack. She was the cat who had not only gotten the cream, but had secured a lifetime supply for the entire feline dynasty.

"Is it not a charming room, Your Grace?" Mama began, her voice shimmering with effort.

The Duke's gaze swept the area with the enthusiasm of a man inspecting for dry rot. "It is a room," he stated.

A brief, pained silence followed. Lady Vexhall, a woman whose face was a testament to the architectural possibilities of powder and rouge, leaped into the breach. "The Duke is a man of discerning taste, Beatrice. He appreciates substance over frivolity. Is that not so, Your Grace?"

"I appreciate order," he replied, his tone suggesting this room possessed none.

I took a sip of my tea and wished it were poison. A small, painless dose, of course. Just enough to grant me a few hours of oblivion.

My performance thus far consisted of smiling. It was a simple role, yet I found it exhausting. My lips felt stiff. I was certain my smile looked more like a pained grimace, the sort one might adopt upon discovering a worm in their apple.

The Duke had said precisely seven words to me in the carriage on the way here. They were: "The traffic on Oxford Street is abysmal." I had agreed that it was, indeed, abysmal. The scintillating conversation had ended there. Now, he seemed determined to break that record for verbosity.

"Araminta, dear," Lady Vexhall chirped, turning her sharp eyes on me. "You are looking radiant. The flush of new love, no doubt."

I felt my practiced smile falter. The only thing flushing me was the proximity of a man who looked at me as if I were a piece of furniture he had begrudgingly acquired. "You are too kind, Lady Vexhall."

"And the ring!" she exclaimed, leaning forward to inspect my hand. "My word. A stone of that size. Thaddeus, you have been most generous."

I noticed she called him Thaddeus. A familiarity I suspected he tolerated rather than enjoyed.

"The Renshawe diamonds are of adequate quality," the Duke said, his voice flat. He made the magnificent ring on my finger sound like a passable turnip.

"Adequate!" my mother breathed, her hand fluttering at her chest. "Your Grace, your modesty is as notable as your generosity."

I did not think he was being modest. I thought he was being precise.

I decided I had to say something. The silence was becoming a living entity, growing larger and more awkward with each passing second. It was my duty, as the future duchess, to slay it.

"Did you see the new bonnets at Madame Dubois's shop window, Mama?" I asked, my voice sounding impossibly frivolous. "They are trimmed with the most extraordinary Venetian lace."

I was discussing millinery with a man who looked as if he had never experienced a moment of frivolity in his life. It was a new circle of hell, one upholstered in chintz.

"How lovely, dear," Mama said, her eyes pleading with me to elicit more than a grunt from my fiancé.

The Duke said nothing. He picked up a scone, inspected it with suspicion, and set it back down on his plate, untouched. The scone looked offended. I knew the feeling.

The drawing room door opened, and a young footman entered, carrying a fresh pot of tea on a silver tray. He was young, no older than sixteen, with a smattering of freckles and a look of sheer terror in his eyes. He moved with the cautious, jerky movements of someone convinced a catastrophe was imminent. It was the sort of expression that often precedes one.

We all watched him. It was impossible not to. His progress across the vast Aubusson carpet was a drama in miniature. He approached our sofa, his hands trembling slightly, causing the fine china to rattle.

My mother's lips thinned. She had an ironclad intolerance for incompetence in servants. It was, in her opinion, a moral failing.

The footman—Finnian, I believed his name was—reached our little island of tension. He leaned forward to place the heavy pot on the low table before us. His hand shook. The lid of the teapot rattled. His eyes widened. He fumbled.

The teapot tipped.

It did not fall to the floor. It tipped sideways on the silver tray, and a gush of steaming, brown tea flooded the polished surface with a sickening splash and clatter.

Finnian froze, his face a mask of pure horror. He looked as though he expected to be hauled off to the Tower immediately.

My mother drew in a sharp, preparatory breath. I knew that sound. It was the preamble to a verbal evisceration, a quiet, controlled, and utterly devastating critique that would leave the poor boy wishing for the sweet release of a public flogging.

But before she could utter a single, soul-crushing syllable, the Duke moved.

It was not a large movement. It was a small, precise, and shockingly swift action. He leaned forward, his body instantly creating a physical barrier, a shield of tailored grey wool between my mother and the terrified footman. His left hand shot out and steadied the pot on the tray, stopping any further spillage.

"A near miss," the Duke stated, his voice perfectly even. There was no anger. No irritation. Nothing. It was a simple statement of fact.

With his other hand, he took a linen napkin from the table. He calmly and efficiently blotted the pool of tea on the tray, his movements economical and clean. The entire incident, from spill to solution, took less than five seconds.

He then looked at Finnian. The boy was still frozen, pale as a sheet.

"See to a fresh pot," the Duke commanded. His tone was not kind. It was not cruel. It was the voice of a man directing a subordinate, expecting to be obeyed without question. It was an order, not a reprimand.

Finnian seemed to break from his trance. "Yes, Your Grace. At once, Your Grace." He picked up the tray, his hands still shaking, and practically fled the room.

My mother's mouth, which had been open to deliver her tirade, closed with a soft click. She looked utterly thwarted.

The Duke settled back against the sofa. He turned his cool gaze upon Lady Vexhall. "You were telling me about the proposed canal bill, my lady. You believe it will not pass the Lords?"

The conversation shifted, pulled by his will into a new, blander channel. The moment was over. The boy was saved. The social fabric, which had threatened to tear, had been smoothly mended without a single raised voice.

I stared at him. I had been watching his face throughout the entire exchange. There had been no flicker of pity for the boy. There had been no warmth, no compassion. There had only been a swift, decisive, and utterly dispassionate management of a chaotic situation.

He had not saved the boy from my mother's wrath out of kindness. He had done it, I suspected, because a public scolding was messy. It was disorderly. It was an inefficient display of emotion, and the Duke, I was beginning to realize, did not tolerate inefficiency. He had not protected the footman. He had managed him.

The realization left me profoundly unsettled. A man who shouted, I could understand. A man who sneered, I could despise. But a man who neutralized a problem with the detached precision of a surgeon resetting a bone was something else entirely. It was not the act of a heartless man. A heartless man would have let my mother have her sport. But it was not the act of a kind one either.

It was the act of a man who craved control above all else. Control of his household, control of his conversations, control of the very atoms in the air around him.

He felt my stare. His grey eyes, cool and remote, shifted to meet mine for a barest second. There was nothing in them. No question. No acknowledgment of what had just passed between us. It was like looking into a deep, still lake on a winter's day. You knew there was a whole world down there, but the surface was frozen solid, and you had no idea what lived, or died, in the depths.

I looked away first, my heart thudding with a strange new rhythm. It was not fear, precisely. It was a profound and unnerving confusion.

Papa had said my fiancé was a cold man. I had believed him. But after today, I suspected he was wrong. Thaddeus Greycourt was not merely cold. He was a fortress, walled and moated, with a single, tightly guarded gate. And I, his future wife, was standing on the outside, with no invitation, and no hope of ever finding a way in.

He was not a monster. He was, perhaps, something far more terrifying. A man I would never, ever understand.

4

An Unexpected Spark

Araminta

L ady Philomena Millicent's annual ball was the undisputed pinnacle of the London season. It was an institution, a grand spectacle of matrimonial ambition and calculated social maneuvering. It was also, I quickly decided, a form of exquisite torture.

The air in the ballroom was thick enough to chew. It was a noxious perfume of sweat, beeswax, and a thousand competing floral scents from the bosoms of hopeful debutantes. Hundreds of candles burned in massive chandeliers overhead, casting a glittering, merciless light on the proceedings. The heat was oppressive. The noise was a physical assault, a cacophony of screeching violins, booming laughter, and the rustle of a king's ransom in silk.

And at the center of it all, I stood beside the Duke of Renshawe. My arm was linked through his. The Renshawe diamonds glittered coldly on my finger and at my throat. I was not a guest. I was an exhibit. *Exhibit A: The Future Duchess.*

Thaddeus was a pillar of ducal fortitude in the chaos. He navigated the crush with an unnerving calm, his handsome face a mask of polite indifference. He performed his duty with grim efficiency. He introduced me to a seemingly endless parade of titled individuals whose names I instantly forgot.

"Lady Araminta, may I present Baron Ormsby."

A stout man with a wheezing laugh and eyes that lingered on my dowry.

"Lady Araminta, the Viscountess Northwood."

A woman with a face so pinched she looked as though she perpetually smelled something foul.

With each introduction, Thaddeus would state my name. He would state their name. He would nod. The transaction would be complete. He spoke to me only to identify the next person in line. He never once asked if I was warm, or if I required a glass of water, or if my head was pounding from the sheer volume of it all. I suspected such trivial human concerns did not occur to him.

We were standing near a potted palm when he was cornered. A portly, red-faced politician, Sir Jasper Plumm, descended upon him with the unstoppable momentum of a runaway boulder.

"Renshawe! Just the man. I must have your thoughts on the proposed Corn Laws amendment," Sir Jasper boomed, spraying a fine mist of spittle into the air.

The Duke turned his full, solemn attention to Sir Jasper. A flicker of something that might have been interest—or at least focused concentration—entered his eyes. It was the most animated I had seen him all evening. He was more engaged by agricultural tariffs than by the woman whose life was now legally bound to his.

This was my chance.

"I find I am in need of some punch, Your Grace," I murmured, my voice a quiet interruption to a riveting discussion of import duties.

He did not look at me. His gaze remained fixed on Sir Jasper. He gave a curt, almost imperceptible nod. Permission granted. Or perhaps, presence dismissed. With him, it was difficult to tell the difference.

I slipped away, my relief so profound it felt like shedding a heavy cloak. I moved through the glittering, chattering throng, a ghost gliding past conversations about court scandals and disastrous new fashions. For the first time all night, I felt my shoulders relax. I felt as though I could breathe. It was this giddy, intoxicating sense of freedom that made me careless.

My focus was on the refreshment table, a distant oasis of claret cup and lemonade. I was navigating a particularly dense cluster of feathered turbans and starched cravats. I took a step backward to avoid colliding with a dowager built like a battleship.

The impact was solid. A man's body. My heel came down on his polished shoe. A gasp went up from those nearby. A splash of crimson liquid—claret cup, I presumed—arched through the air in a perfect, horrifying parabola.

"Good heavens!" a man's voice exclaimed. It was a rich, amused baritone, not an angry one. "A direct hit! My waistcoat is mortally wounded."

I spun around, my face burning with a mortification so complete it was paralyzing. "Oh, forgive me! I am so terribly sorry, I did not see..."

My words trailed off. My apology died in my throat.

He was magnificent.

He stood dabbing at the large, dripping stain on his pristine white silk waistcoat. He was tall, with a cascade of unruly dark hair that defied the era's fashion for severe styling. But it was his eyes that captured me. They were the color of warm hazel, flecked with gold, and they were positively alight with a wild, irrepressible amusement. A roguish grin played on his lips. Where the Duke was a statue carved from cold marble, this man was a living, breathing wildfire.

Seeing the horror on my face, his expression softened instantly. He took a half-step closer, subtly shielding me from the curious onlookers. His voice dropped, becoming a reassuring murmur meant only for me. "Please do not look so alarmed. My tailor will weep for a week, but I assure you, I will recover. The honor of being so spectacularly targeted by the loveliest woman in the room is more than enough to soothe my wounded pride."

His words wrapped around me, a warm and comforting blanket over my sudden panic. He was not laughing *at* me. He was inviting me into a joke, making us conspirators. A laugh escaped me, a genuine, surprised bark of amusement that felt rusty in my own throat.

"I assure you, sir, I am not in the habit of assaulting gentlemen's waist-coats," I managed, my own lips twitching into an unfamiliar shape. A smile.

His grin widened, and it was a devastating thing. "A pity," he sighed, his voice a low, intimate hum. "For a moment, I thought I had been singled out for a rare honor indeed. Evander Greycourt, at your service. And, I see, entirely at your mercy."

Greycourt.

The name landed not like a stone, but like a bolt of lightning. It electrified the air between us. My smile froze. How? How could this man—this creature of warmth and laughter and vibrant, reassuring life—be related to the cold, silent man I was promised to? It was a paradox. A cosmic joke. It was impossible. Thaddeus moved through the world as if it were a problem to be solved. This man moved through it as if it were a grand, wonderful adventure he was inviting you to join. *How can a person like this exist in the same family?*

"You are... the Duke's brother," I stated, my voice a faint whisper of disbelief.

"The very same," he confirmed, his eyes dancing with a light that seemed to say he understood my shock completely. "The spare, not the heir. The scandal, not the sermon. And you," he said, his gaze dropping for a mere second to the enormous diamond on my finger before returning to my face, locking me in place, "unless I am much mistaken, are the beautiful and brave Lady Araminta Wexley. My future sister-in-law."

He took my hand. His skin was warm, his grip confident and alive. He did not just brush my knuckles in the formal style. He turned my hand over, his thumb stroking the sensitive skin of my wrist for a bare, shocking second before his lips met my glove. It was not a salute. It was a claim. The touch was not a jolt; it was a conflagration, a sudden, roaring heat in the frozen landscape of my life.

He straightened, his eyes still holding mine, still full of that wild, knowing warmth. "It is an absolute pleasure to finally meet the woman brave enough to take on Thaddeus," he said, his voice dropping into a conspiratorial murmur that made me feel like we were the only two people in the room.

The introduction was a spark that lit a fuse. It was not just humor and life. It was a profound, instant connection. A shared, secret understanding that crackled in the air between us. He didn't just see a future duchess. He saw a woman in a gilded cage, and he was, with a single, devastating smile, offering to show her the sky.

As I looked into Evander Greycourt's laughing hazel eyes, I felt my first genuine smile in what felt like a lifetime spread across my face. It was a dangerous, thrilling, and utterly unexpected feeling. And I knew, with a certainty that both terrified and exhilarated me, that I was in very, very deep trouble.

5

Banter and Beguilement

Araminta

I pulled my hand from his grasp, though the warmth of his touch lingered on my skin, a phantom sensation that was both alarming and pleasant. I had to regain my footing. I was the future Duchess of Renshawe. I was not some giddy debutante to be flustered by a handsome face and a charming line. My entire future, and my family's, depended on my composure.

"Brave?" I repeated, my voice cooler than I felt. My composure was a shield I raised hastily. "I believe 'dutiful' is the more appropriate term, my lord."

"Ah, but duty in the face of such crushing boredom is the highest form of bravery," Evander countered. His gaze did not leave my face, and he had the unnerving habit of looking at me as if he were genuinely listening, a novel experience after an hour with his brother. His eyes swept the glittering ballroom with an air of profound amusement. "Especially in a room so thick with pomposity you could cut it with a cake knife. You deserve a medal for this evening alone. Or at the very least," he added, his voice dropping, "a man to tell you that your courage is far more captivating than your compliance."

The words were so direct, so personal, it felt as if he had peeled back the layers of my careful performance and seen the weary woman beneath. A laugh bubbled up before I could suppress it. I disguised it as a cough, pressing my

18

glove to my lips. It was a poor effort. His grin told me he was not fooled.

"You are terribly improper, Lord Evander," I chided, the words lacking any real heat.

"Impropriety?" he said, his voice a low, musical hum that vibrated through the air between us. "My dear Lady Araminta, it is not a talent. It is a carefully cultivated art form. While my brother was learning how to count his estates, I was learning how to count the ways a woman's eyes light up just before she laughs. I dare say my education was far more rewarding, and has left me with considerably fewer headaches."

He was a whirlwind. A charming, wild, and utterly impossible man. He spoke of seduction as if it were a scholarly pursuit, and the worst part was, I felt myself becoming his most willing subject. My mind reeled. How could a person like this exist?

He looked down at the large crimson stain on his chest. He wore an expression of such theatrical mourning that I could no longer contain myself. A real giggle escaped. It was a light, airy sound I scarcely recognized as my own. I felt a hot blush creep up my neck. I was giggling. With my fiancé's brother. The sheer, dizzying impropriety of it was a thrill.

"Perhaps salt and cool water will remedy the injury," I suggested, my voice still shaky with suppressed mirth.

"An excellent prescription," he straightened up, his eyes gleaming with a predatory charm. "But a tedious one. I have a much better idea. A lady should not have to suffer such a dull party without proper fortification. And you, my dear Lady Araminta, are clearly dying of terminal respectability. Allow me to rescue you with a glass of punch. Think of it as a brief, delicious escape. No one will even notice you are gone." He leaned an inch closer, his voice dropping to a husky whisper that was pure temptation. "Except me."

My mind screamed all the appropriate warnings. I should thank him for his humor, curtsey politely, and march directly back to Thaddeus's side. I should return to my post. But the thought of resuming my vigil beside the human pillar of duty was so bleak, so utterly soul-crushing, that my will to be proper crumbled into dust.

"Very well, my lord," I heard myself agree. A thrill of pure rebellion shot through me. It was terrifying. It was wonderful. "But only if you promise that your wardrobe will not suffer any further casualties on my account."

"You have my solemn vow," he said, placing a hand over his heart. "Though I make no promises about my own clumsiness. It is a vital part of my charm, or so I am told."

He offered me his arm. I hesitated for only a second before placing my fingertips upon his sleeve. His arm was warm and solid beneath the fine wool of his coat. As he led me away, I risked a glance over my shoulder. Thaddeus had not moved. He was still deep in his conversation about tariffs, oblivious. Or so I prayed.

Evander led me not toward the main refreshment table, which was swarmed by a throng of thirsty guests, but to a smaller, secondary station tucked away in an alcove. The location was more secluded, shielded by a large marble pillar. It offered a perfect vantage point from which to observe the grand theater of the ball without being at its center. It felt like a deliberate, strategic retreat. It felt like a conspiracy.

He handed me a crystal cup of lemonade, his fingers brushing mine in a way that felt anything but accidental. He secured a glass of claret for himself, holding it up to the light. "To new acquaintances," he said, his eyes meeting mine over the rim of his glass. "And to brief, delicious escapes."

"To... escapes," I echoed, taking a small, nervous sip. The lemonade was tart and sweet. It did little to cool the heat in my cheeks.

We stood together in the relative quiet of the alcove. From here, the ballroom was a stage, and its players were all performing their parts with gusto. For the first time all night, I felt like a member of the audience, not a player under the hot glare of the footlights.

"Before we begin our critique of the local fauna," Evander said, his tone shifting from playful to something more serious, "tell me something true, Lady Araminta."

I blinked, taken aback. "True?"

"Yes. A true thing. Not what the weather is doing, or your opinion on the music. Something that is actually real. For instance," he leaned against the pillar, the picture of casual grace, "outside of being dutiful and brave, what is

20

it that you truly enjoy?"

The question was so simple, so direct, so utterly personal, that it completely disarmed me. No one had asked me a question like that in years. Not my mother, not my father, and certainly not the Duke. They cared about what I represented, not what I enjoyed. I opened my mouth to give a standard, polite answer—needlepoint, reading, walking—but the words felt like lies. He would know they were lies.

"I... I am not certain I remember," I confessed in a small voice.

His expression softened with a sympathy that made my heart ache. "Then we shall have to make it our mission to find out," he said gently. "But for now, let us return to the much easier sport of mocking our betters. Look there," he murmured, his voice once again low and close to my ear. He nodded subtly toward a man across the room. "Lord Alistair Finch. He believes that standing with his chest puffed out makes him look powerful. What it really does is announce to the entire room that his tailor had to let out his waistcoat after luncheon."

I choked on my lemonade. Laughter sputtered from me, sharp and sudden. I pressed my handkerchief to my mouth, my eyes watering.

"You are wicked," I whispered, once I could breathe again.

"I am observant," he corrected smoothly. "It is a different thing entirely. And see Lady Plumwell? The one with the enormous, trembling feather in her hair?"

I glanced at the woman in question. Her turban was a marvel of engineering, a towering creation of silk and ostrich feathers that shuddered with every slight movement of her head.

"It is said," Evander continued, his voice laced with mischief, "that she hides sherry-soaked biscuits in her hairpiece for emergencies. Her husband is famously dull. Emergencies are frequent."

"You cannot possibly know that," I gasped, scandalized and delighted in equal measure.

"My dear Lady Araminta," he said with a dramatic sigh, "knowing things for a fact is so rarely enjoyable. Imagining them is much better. Otherwise, she is just a woman in a ridiculous hat. This way, she is a heroine on a secret, sherry-fueled adventure. Much more compelling, do you not agree?"

I found myself looking at the grand, stuffy personages of the *ton* in a completely new light. Through his eyes, they were not intimidating arbiters of social standing. They were characters in a grand, absurd comedy. Our shared commentary was a secret language spoken in whispers and laughter. The chemistry between us was an undeniable current, a low hum of energy that felt more real than anything else in the room.

Then my gaze drifted across the room and landed on my fiancé.

Thaddeus was still deep in conversation with Sir Jasper. His back was to me. He stood as still as stone, a dark, unmoving figure in the swirling sea of color and motion. He was the embodiment of all the duty and seriousness that I had, for a few blissful moments, managed to forget.

The guilt was a sudden, sharp stab. It was a cold splash of water on a warm, pleasant dream. My smile faltered. The laughter died in my throat. The diamond on my finger suddenly felt heavy, a cold weight of accusation. This was wrong. This was improper. This was a betrayal.

Evander noticed the shift instantly. His teasing tone vanished. "What is it?" he asked softly, his voice full of concern. "What do you see?"

I could not answer. I could only stare at the unmoving figure of my future.

Evander followed my gaze. He saw his brother. A strange expression, a mix of frustration and something like pity, crossed his face. He turned back to me, his voice low. "Look at him," he said, not unkindly. "He is not enjoying this ball. He is auditing it. I imagine he is mentally calculating the cost of the wax per minute and drafting a report on how to improve its efficiency by seventeen percent."

My heart gave a nervous, painful leap. But his words were so true. A tiny, traitorous giggle escaped me. It was a small, breathy sound, but in our alcove, it sounded as loud as a thunderclap. My eyes flew to his, wide with alarm at my own audacity.

Evander's expression was no longer teasing. It was soft, almost gentle. "Severe is Thaddeus's natural state," he said, his voice holding no malice, only a note of sad resignation. "He was born with a furrow in his brow and a list of responsibilities in his fist. It is my solemn fraternal duty to try and un-furrow it from time to time. A task at which I fail spectacularly."

His gaze met mine. The shared, secret joke about his brother felt shockingly, dangerously intimate. It was a confidence, a shared truth that bound us together in that moment. The excitement and the guilt warred within me, a dizzying, chaotic battle.

I looked at this man, this Lord Evander Greycourt, with his laughing eyes and his easy charm. In the space of one evening, he had made me laugh. He had made me feel clever and seen and alive. He had treated me not as a future duchess, not as a contractual obligation, but as a person. He had asked me what I enjoyed.

The realization hit me with the force of a physical blow. I had felt more alive in this single hour than I had since the day my father's debts had become a chain around my neck. The life I had resigned myself to—a quiet, orderly, passionless existence as the Duchess of Renshawe—suddenly seemed like a slow, suffocating death.

And the man offering me a glimpse of life was the one man in all of England I could not, must not, have.

6

Forbidden Laughter

Araminta

The realization struck me with the force of a physical blow. I had felt more alive in this single hour than I had in the entire month since my life was signed away in my father's library. The thought was a stone dropped into the placid, miserable pool of my acceptance. The ripples were spreading, and they were threatening to become a tidal wave.

My smile must have vanished. The light, easy mood between us evaporated, leaving a sudden, charged silence in its wake. Evander's charming expression shifted instantly. The teasing glint in his hazel eyes was replaced by a look of sharp, genuine concern. He tilted his head, studying my face with an intensity that made me feel utterly transparent.

"I have said something to offend," he stated. It was not a question. It was a soft, regretful conclusion.

"No," I said, my voice too quick, too sharp. My carefully constructed composure was cracking. "Of course not. It is only..." I faltered, searching for a shield, an excuse, anything to hide behind. "It is terribly warm in here."

It was the truth, but it was also a profound lie. The heat of the room was nothing compared to the sudden, suffocating heat of my own internal chaos.

Evander looked at me for a long moment, and I had the unnerving feeling he could see straight through my flimsy excuse. A slow, knowing smile touched his lips. "Is that what we are calling it?" he murmured, his voice a low, intimate hum. "I thought it was the crushing weight of a thousand expectations sucking the very air from the room." He glanced toward the far end of the ballroom where a set of tall French doors stood open, leading out into the velvet darkness. "A prison, no matter how prettily gilded, is still a prison. Would you care for a moment of parole, Lady Araminta?"

His offer was not just for fresh air. It was for escape. A brief, delicious, and utterly scandalous escape. My mind, the sensible, dutiful part of me that had governed my actions for weeks, screamed a resounding *No*. To slip away, alone, into a dark garden with my fiancé's brother was a deliberate step over a line from which there could be no return. It was reckless. It was ruinous.

But my heart, that foolish, traitorous, and suddenly wide-awake organ, was pounding out a desperate, frantic *Yes*. It yearned for the cool air. It yearned for five more minutes of this man's company. It yearned to feel alive, just for a moment longer.

My heart won. It was not even a fair fight.

"Perhaps for just a moment," I conceded, my voice a low murmur. I could not quite meet his eyes. I was afraid of the triumphant, knowing sparkle he would find in mine.

"A moment is all it takes," he whispered, a promise in his tone. He offered his arm again. This time, when I took it, I was acutely aware of the impropriety. Every eye in the ballroom felt like it was on us as we moved toward the doors. It was an illusion, of course. No one was paying us any mind. But my conscience was a harsh spotlight, and I felt utterly exposed. The muscle in his arm was firm and warm beneath my gloved fingertips. It was the arm of a man who rode horses, not one who spent his days shuffling papers. It felt like an anchor in a storm, and I was not at all certain whether he was pulling me to safety or dragging me down into the depths.

We stepped through the doors and onto a wide stone terrace. The change in atmosphere was immediate and profound. The oppressive heat of the ballroom gave way to a cool, gentle breeze that felt like heaven against my flushed cheeks. The cacophony of the orchestra softened, the music now a muted, romantic melody drifting on the night air. The garden below was a labyrinth of shadows and silver, bathed in the cool light of a full moon.

"See?" Evander said softly, his voice a pleasant rumble beside me. "Freedom. Much better than perfume and pomposity, is it not?"

He led me down a short flight of stone steps and into the garden proper. We strolled along a gravel path, our footsteps a quiet crunch in the stillness. The scent of roses was thick and sweet, mingling with the clean, damp fragrance of the dew-kissed leaves. We were alone. Utterly, completely, and dangerously alone.

"And what are you thinking about now, my lord?" I asked, my voice quieter here. The garden seemed to demand a certain reverence. "In this newfound freedom."

He stopped walking, turning to face me in a pool of moonlight. The playful humor was gone from his face, replaced by a raw sincerity that was far more potent. "I am thinking," he said, his voice soft, "that I have just witnessed a miracle."

I blinked. "A miracle?"

"Your laugh," he said, his gaze intense. "Not the polite one you use in drawing rooms. The real one. It came out a moment ago, in that stuffy little alcove, like a bird from a cage. And I am thinking," he took a half-step closer, his presence seeming to consume all the air around us, "that it is a profound tragedy that my brother, who owns your future, has likely never heard it. But I have."

His words were not a compliment. They were a claim. They were a quiet declaration that he had seen a part of me that Thaddeus had not. That he valued a part of me that Thaddeus did not even know existed. I had no reply. I could only look at him, my heart a confused, aching tangle of pleasure and guilt. This was the man who saw my laughter as a miracle. My own fiancé saw me as a sensible arrangement.

He must have seen the turmoil in my eyes. With a deft change of mood, his playful grin returned, though the intensity still lingered in his gaze. He spotted a nearby trellis heavy with pale, white blossoms. He stepped over to it and, with a flourish, plucked a single, perfect rose from its stem.

He turned back to me. He did not bow this time. He stepped close, so close that the moonlight could not slip between us. His knuckles brushed against the silk of my gown at my waist, a feather-light touch that sent a bolt of heat through my entire body. "A spoil of war," he murmured, his voice a husky whisper. "For the woman who so thoroughly conquered the evening."

He lifted the rose, but he did not hand it to me. Instead, he reached for my hand. He took my gloved fingers in his, his touch warm and firm. With his other hand, he gently, deliberately, tucked the stem of the rose into the delicate lacing of my evening glove, securing it at my wrist. His fingers brushed against my skin, warm and slightly rough, the touch of a man who lived in the world, not just observed it. It was a brief, shocking moment of skin against skin. An intimacy so unexpected, so forbidden, it felt more profound than a kiss.

The touch was an electric shock to my system. All my carefully constructed walls, all my resolves, all my fears, they all turned to dust.

A laugh escaped me.

It was not a giggle. It was not a chuckle. It was a deep, unrestrained, and utterly joyous sound that seemed to rise up from the very core of my being. It was the sound of a prisoner tasting freedom for the first time. The sound of a soul remembering it could sing. I threw my head back and laughed at the moon, at the stars, at the sheer, impossible wonder of this man.

And in the echo of that laugh, as I looked at him, at the triumphant, tender smile on his face, the realization hit me with the force of a physical blow.

It was a flash of lightning, illuminating the dark, lonely prison I had been living in.

When was the last time?

When had a man looked at me as if I were a miracle? When had a touch, so simple, so fleeting, ever made me feel so completely, incandescently alive?

The answer was never.

The realization was a sharp, physical pain, a sudden and unwelcome grief for the life I had not known I was missing. The beautiful, forbidden laughter that still warmed my cheeks now made my heart ache with a sorrow so profound it stole my breath. It was the sound of my own soul, and I had not heard its voice in months.

That laughter, that touch, shared under the stars with a man who was not my betrothed, had revealed a terrible, undeniable truth. My engagement was not just a passionless arrangement. It was a cage. And I had been slowly, silently suffocating inside it. Something was wrong. Something was fundamentally, terribly wrong with the life I had so dutifully accepted.

And I knew, with a certainty that was both terrifying and thrilling, that I could never, ever go back to pretending I did not know it.

7

Seeds of Rebellion

Araminta

The journey home from Lady Millicent's ball was a silent, suffocating affair. The Duke sat across from me in the carriage, a dark shape against the fleeting gaslights of London. The memory of my own laughter in the garden felt like a crime I had just committed, and this carriage was my tumbrel, carrying me away from the scene. I stared resolutely at my own hands, twisted together in my lap, praying he would not speak to me, praying he would not look at me. I wanted to be invisible.

For ten minutes, my prayer was answered. The only sounds were the rumble of the wheels on the cobblestones and the rhythmic clip-clop of the horses' hooves. Thaddeus was as still and silent as stone, his profile a rigid line against the window. He seemed to be, as usual, in a world of his own, one composed of ledgers and logic.

Then, he spoke.

"The evening was not to your satisfaction, Lady Araminta?"

The question, dropped into the profound silence, was so unexpected it was like a physical shock. My head snapped up. I stared at him, my heart leaping into my throat. He was looking at me. Not through me, not at the wall behind my head, but directly at me. His grey eyes were unreadable in the flickering, uncertain light of the passing lamps, but they were focused entirely on my face.

It was the first question he had ever asked me about my own feelings. And it terrified me.

What did he mean? Had he seen something? Had my laughter been so loud it had carried from the garden? Had someone commented on my long absence with his brother? My mind raced, a frantic scramble of guilt and fear.

"No, Your Grace," I stammered, my voice a stranger's. I cleared my throat, forcing a polite, placid tone. "The evening was splendid. Lady Millicent is a remarkable hostess."

It was the correct answer. A safe, meaningless social nicety.

He considered my reply, his gaze unwavering. It did not feel like a shared moment. It felt like an interrogation. He was a scientist observing a specimen, noting my flushed cheeks, my too-quick reply, my inability to meet his eyes for more than a second.

"You seemed... distracted," he stated. It was a simple observation, yet it carried the weight of an accusation. He had noticed. While I had thought him oblivious, lost in his world of tariffs, he had been observing me.

"The heat, Your Grace," I said quickly, grasping for the same flimsy excuse I had used with Evander. "It can be overwhelming."

"I see."

Two words. They conveyed nothing and everything. He held my gaze for another long, unnerving moment. I felt pinned in place, my every nervous tremor, every guilty thought, laid bare for his cool inspection.

Then, as quickly as it had begun, it was over. He gave a single, curt nod. He turned his head and resumed his silent contemplation of the London streets. The door was shut. The moment of connection—if it could even be called that—was gone.

The silence that returned was a thousand times worse than before. It was no longer a simple absence of conversation. It was a watchful, knowing silence. He was not just a cold statue. He was a thinking, observing man. And he had seen something in me tonight that had prompted him to break his own rules. The thought was more frightening than any open anger. It left me feeling exposed and utterly, completely alone.

My bedroom, when I finally reached it, felt different. It was the same room I had left hours before, with its familiar cream-and-blue furnishings and the scent of lavender from the linens. But I had changed. The room had not. It now felt too small, its elegant walls a pretty, confining box.

I dismissed my lady's maid, Eliza, with a quiet word, needing to be alone. Her knowing, worried eyes followed me as she left, but she asked no questions. Some disasters are too fresh for examination.

Alone, I unclasped the Renshawe diamonds from my throat. The necklace was heavy and cold. It felt like a chain. I placed it in its velvet box and snapped the lid shut. Then, my movements slow and deliberate, I drew the diamond engagement ring from my finger. I set it on the polished surface of my dressing table. It sat there under the soft glow of the oil lamp, a brilliant, accusing eye. A star of immense value and no warmth whatsoever.

My gloved fingers went to the single object I had carried home from the ball. The white rose. It was still tucked into the sash of my gown. I drew it out. Its petals were cool and soft against my skin, like a whispered promise. I lifted it to my face and inhaled. It smelled of night air and damp earth and a faint, indefinable scent that was purely Evander. It was the scent of life.

I held the rose in one hand and stared at the ring with the other. My choice. My future. A flower that would wilt by morning versus a stone that would outlast empires. One was a fleeting moment of pure, unadulterated joy. The other was a lifetime of respectable, orderly security. A prison of perfect, unyielding permanence.

I sank onto the small stool before my dressing table, my ballgown pooling around me like a silver cloud. I could not stop my mind from replaying the evening. It was a relentless projector, casting images against the dark screen of my memory.

I saw Evander's laughing eyes as he surrendered to my clumsy assault. I heard the rich, warm timbre of his voice as he teased me about Lord Finch's pigeon-like posture. I felt the conspiratorial warmth of his arm under my fingertips, the way he leaned in close to share a wicked observation, his breath a ghost against my ear. These memories were vivid and Technicolor, saturated

31

with a life I had not realized I was missing. They made my heart ache with a feeling that was equal parts pleasure and profound loss.

This joy, this forbidden spark, was immediately followed by the cold shadow of guilt. My internal monologue was a stern governess, rapping my knuckles for my disgraceful behavior. *You are betrothed. You are to be a duchess. You stood in the dark with another man. You laughed with him. You let him touch your hand.*

The chastisement was sharp, but it was surprisingly ineffective. Because immediately after the guilt came another set of images, these rendered in shades of grey.

I saw the Duke. I saw him standing beside me, a handsome, silent statue. I saw his cool, dismissive nod when I asked for punch. I saw his back, ramrod straight, as he discussed agricultural policy with Sir Jasper. But now there was a new image. His cool grey eyes, studying me in the flickering light of the carriage. His quiet, probing questions. He was not just an asset manager. He was a warden, quietly observing the behavior of his prisoner.

I had accepted this. I had told myself it was part of the bargain. A cold husband was a small price to pay for my family's salvation. I had prepared myself for a life of quiet dignity, of managing a great household, of producing an heir. I had believed it would be enough.

I had been a fool.

Evander's warmth had not just beguiled me. It had exposed a painful, undeniable truth. It had held a lamp up to my arrangement with the Duke, and in its glow, I saw the absolute, desolate emptiness of it. There was no spark with Thaddeus. There was no connection. There was no laughter. There was only the cold, hard reality of a contract, overseen by a watchful, silent guard.

A question, small and sharp as a needle, pricked at the edge of my consciousness.

Could I do it?

Could I truly spend the next fifty years of my life beside a man who looked at me not with indifference, but with a cool, assessing scrutiny? Could I wake each morning and go to sleep each night in a house ruled by orderly silence? Could I watch myself wither, my spirit shrinking day by day, until the girl who had laughed in the garden was nothing but a faint, ghostly memory? Could I become a woman who housed her sherry in her hat because it was the only pleasure she had left?

The thought was so horrifying it made my stomach clench.

But duty. The word was a drumbeat in my blood. Duty to my father, whose face, etched with shame and relief, was a constant image in my mind. Duty to my mother, whose social ambitions now rested entirely on my shoulders. Duty to my younger sisters, whose futures depended on the advantageous match I was making. To falter now was not just to fail myself. It was to fail all of them. It was to plunge my family back into the ruin from which this marriage was our only escape. My sacrifice was their salvation. I had no right to question the terms.

I stood up and began to pace the confines of my room. The silver silk of my gown whispered against the carpet, a restless, unhappy sound. I was trapped. I was caught between an impossible duty and an unbearable future.

I stopped before the window and looked out at the sleeping city. The moon was high and bright, the same moon that had illuminated the garden, that had witnessed my forbidden laughter.

And then, another thought came. It was smaller than the first, quieter, and infinitely more dangerous. It was a tiny, treacherous whisper from the deepest, most honest part of my soul.

What if I didn't?

What if I didn't marry him?

The thought was so shocking, so utterly seditious, that I gasped. I pressed my hand to my mouth as if to physically force the thought back into the darkness from which it had sprung. It was unthinkable. It was ruinous. It was impossible.

I turned away from the window, my heart hammering against my ribs. I looked at the ring on my dressing table. For the first time, I did not see the salvation of the Wexley name. I did not see the pride in my mother's eyes or the relief on my father's face.

I saw the bars of a cage. A beautiful, brilliant, and inescapable cage.

And the rose, sitting beside it, was a glimpse of the sky outside.

33

I quickly, almost violently, rejected the thought. I was being foolish. I was being hysterical. I was a romantic girl swayed by a charming rogue. My path was set. It was my duty, and I would do it. I would be the Duchess of Renshawe. I would be a good wife. I would learn to find contentment in my orderly, silent world.

But even as I repeated the words to myself like a prayer, I knew they were a lie.

The seed of doubt had been planted. It was a tiny, dark thing, but it had taken root in the fertile ground of my unhappiness. It was there now, lodged deep in my heart, and I knew, with a terrifying certainty, that it would grow. My obedience, once a solid and unshakeable foundation, was beginning to crack.

I picked up the rose. I walked to the washstand, poured fresh water into a crystal glass, and placed the stem inside. It was an act of preservation. An act of rebellion. An act of keeping that one, perfect moment of life alive, if only for a few more days.

I lay awake for hours, staring into the darkness. The path forward, which had once seemed so clear and straight, was now a fractured, uncertain thing. And for the first time since my engagement began, I was not afraid of the Duke's coldness. I was afraid of the burgeoning, terrifying warmth inside myself.

8

Stolen Glances

Araminta

My resolve to behave was a fragile, brittle thing. It was a New Year's resolution made in a moment of panic, destined to be broken before the week was out. I had spent the seven days since Lady Millicent's ball in a state of virtuous self-denial. I had read edifying books on household management. I had practiced my watercolors, painting pale, lifeless landscapes that perfectly reflected my mood. I had accompanied my mother on a series of crushingly dull morning calls, where I smiled and nodded and spoke of the weather with the animation of a porcelain doll. I had been the very model of a dutiful, engaged young woman. I had not allowed myself to think of hazel eyes or forbidden laughter.

It was, without question, the most boring week of my life.

The next test of my resolve came in the form of a garden party at the estate of the Baron and Baroness Fitzharding. The day was deceptively beautiful. The sun shone with a gentle warmth, the sky was a perfect, cloudless blue, and the Baroness's famed rose gardens were in magnificent bloom. It was a perfect setting for polite conversation, lukewarm punch, and simmering social anxiety.

I stood beside the Duke, my hand resting lightly on his arm. His presence was a familiar weight, a cool and steadying force that felt more like an anchor than a comfort. He wore his usual expression of faint, intellectual disdain for his surroundings. He looked at the vibrant, blooming garden as if it were a poorly organized ledger, finding fault with its chaotic explosion of color. We were an island of cool grey in a sea of pastel silks and bright summer bonnets.

My eyes had a will of their own.

I fought them. I truly did. I focused on a particularly large bee hovering near Lady Ashworth's formidable hat. I studied the pattern of the wrought-iron bench across the lawn. I stared at the Duke's impeccably polished shoes, counting the eyelets on his boots. But it was no use. My gaze was a traitor, a magnetic needle seeking its true north. Inevitably, it found him.

Evander.

He was standing near the lemonade table, holding court with a small circle of admirers, including the flighty Miss Calliope Finch. He was not speaking to them so much as performing for them. He gestured with his hands, telling some doubtlessly outrageous story. Laughter erupted from the group. He looked like the sun-drenched, carefree heart of the party. He was everything his brother was not. He was life itself, rendered in waistcoat and breeches.

My heart gave a painful lurch. I forced myself to look away, turning my attention to a stilted conversation Thaddeus was having with an elderly bishop about church finances. I feigned interest. I smiled. I nodded. But after a minute, my treacherous eyes slid sideways again.

Evander had extricated himself from his admirers and was now leaning against a tree, speaking with a friend. The laughter was gone, replaced by a more serious, intent expression as he listened. Even in repose, he radiated a warmth and vitality that seemed to draw all the light in the garden toward him.

As if he could feel my stare, he looked up. Across the manicured lawn, across the heads of fifty gossiping members of the *ton*, his eyes met mine.

The world seemed to hush for a moment. The chatter of the party faded to a dull roar. He gave me a slow, secret smile. It was not the wide, charming grin he gave the world. This was something else. It was a private, shared thing, a spark sent across a crowded space, meant only for me. *I see you,* it said. *Do you see me?*

A jolt, sharp and electric, shot through me. A hot blush flooded my cheeks. I felt it creep up my neck, a flag of my own betrayal. I quickly snapped my head back toward the bishop, my heart hammering against my ribs. I stared intently at a plate of tiny sandwiches on a nearby table, as if they were the most fascinating objects I had ever beheld. I had been caught. I had been caught looking.

"Are you quite well, Lady Araminta?" the Duke's voice asked from beside me. It was a cool, detached sound that sliced through my flustered state.

"Perfectly well, Your Grace," I said, my voice a little too bright.

"Your color is high," he observed, his eyes scanning my face with a dispassionate scrutiny. "I trust the sun is not too strong for you."

It was not a question of concern. It was a diagnosis. He was noting the symptom, the blush, and assigning it a logical cause. He did not suspect the true cause, but the fact that he was looking so closely sent a fresh wave of panic through me.

"No, Your Grace," I lied, fanning my face with my hand for effect. "It is merely pleasant to be out of the city."

"Indeed." He seemed to accept this, but his gaze drifted out across the lawn, lingering for a moment in the exact direction of the lemonade table. His expression was, as always, unreadable. But I felt a sudden, chilling certainty that he had missed nothing. He was a man who noticed when things were out of place. And I, at that moment, was dangerously out of place.

"The Baron's collection of Roman antiquities is said to be noteworthy," he stated, his tone flat, changing the subject without acknowledging the tension. "We should view it."

"Of course, Your Grace," I murmured, allowing him to steer me toward the house. It felt less like a suggestion and more like a strategic retreat, removing me from the field of battle before I could commit any further acts of treason.

Later that afternoon, a game of croquet was proposed. It was the sort of genteel, leisurely activity deemed appropriate for mixed company. It was also, I discovered, an excellent opportunity for chaos and clandestine maneuvering.

The Duke, to my immense relief, declined to play. He cited a desire to discuss

37

some political matter with our host. He stood on the edge of the lawn, a dark, watchful sentinel, as the teams were chosen. I found myself on a team with the aforementioned Miss Calliope Finch and a florid-faced gentleman, Mr. Peregrine Shaw, whose primary athletic accomplishment seemed to be his ability to sweat profusely in even the mildest weather.

Evander, naturally, was on the opposing team. He greeted his selection with a theatrical groan. "I am pitted against my future sister? What a cruel twist of fate. How can I possibly bring my best effort to bear against a member of my own family?"

"Somehow, my lord, I suspect you will manage," I retorted, my voice dry.

His eyes twinkled. "You wound me, Lady Araminta. My loyalty is my finest quality."

The game began. It was a slow, meandering affair. Mr. Shaw, on his first turn, swung his mallet with the force of a blacksmith, sending his ball rocketing past all the wickets and into a prize-winning rosebush. He spent the next five minutes apologizing to a furious Baroness Ashworth. Miss Finch, for her part, seemed more interested in flirting with a young officer observing from the sidelines than in striking her ball at all.

The Duke was drawn into conversation by a stern-looking dowager, his back momentarily turned to the playing field. It was the opening Evander had been waiting for.

My turn came. I stood over my blue ball, attempting to calculate the angle needed to send it through the next wicket. Evander strolled over, ostensibly to retrieve his own ball, which, through a stroke of what I was sure was calculated clumsiness, had landed suspiciously close to mine.

"A challenging shot," he murmured, his voice a low vibration meant only for me. He stood closer than propriety allowed, so close I could feel the warmth radiating from his body. His sleeve brushed against my arm. The fleeting contact was enough to make my pulse skitter.

"I am aware," I said, trying to keep my voice steady. My hand was suddenly slick on the handle of the mallet.

"You are holding it as if it's a venomous snake," he whispered, a laugh in his voice. "It does not bite, I assure you. Though Mr. Shaw's ball did seem to attack that poor rosebush with unprovoked aggression."

A giggle escaped me. I smothered it, turning it into a cough and hiding my mouth behind my gloved hand. I could feel his grin without even looking at him. Just then, I felt a prickling sensation on the back of my neck. I risked a glance toward the spectators. The Duke had turned his head. He was watching us.

My heart froze. I instinctively took a half-step away from Evander.

Evander, without missing a beat, raised his voice slightly. "So you see, Lady Araminta, the trick is to strike it firmly, but not with the force of a charging rhinoceros, as our friend Mr. Shaw demonstrated." His performance was seamless. He made our intimate moment look like a simple, public piece of instruction. He was dangerously good at this.

I nodded, my throat tight, and turned my attention back to my ball as the Duke resumed his conversation.

"The key," Evander continued, his voice dropping back to a low, intimate murmur, "is to abandon all dignity from the start. It makes the inevitable failure much less painful. Aim for the wicket, by all means. But enjoy the journey, even if it ends in ignominy among the petunias."

"Is that your life's philosophy, my lord?" I asked, daring a quick glance at him. His eyes were bright with amusement and something deeper, something that made my stomach flutter.

"In all things," he confirmed with a solemn nod. He looked directly at me, and I knew he was no longer talking about croquet. "Especially the important ones."

He offered a pointer, his hand gesturing toward the wicket. The movement was an excuse to lean even closer. I could smell the clean, sun-warmed scent of his linen coat and the faint, familiar aroma of sandalwood. The world seemed to narrow to this small, charged space around us. The chatter of the party, the distant laughter, it all faded away. There was only the green grass, the warm sun, and the dangerous, exhilarating presence of this man beside me.

I took my shot. My hand was unsteady. The mallet connected with a dull thud. The ball rolled forward, pathetically, and stopped a full two feet short of the wicket.

"A valiant effort," Evander declared loudly, for the benefit of anyone watching. Then he added in a whisper, for my ears only, "A truly abysmal shot. But you looked magnificent doing it."

My face was on fire. I could feel a smile, a real, unrestrained smile, blooming on my lips. I hid it by turning away to watch the next player. Each time it was his turn, he would find a reason to pass by me. Each time, a whispered witticism, a shared glance, a fleeting, accidental touch. Each interaction was a small, secret treasure, a stolen jewel of joy in the vast, dull vault of my betrothal. It was a thrilling, terrifying game played in plain sight.

The game finally concluded. My team had lost spectacularly. I did not care in the slightest. I was giddy, my heart racing, my blood singing with a dangerous, forbidden energy.

I turned to walk back toward the spectators. And my gaze collided with the Duke's.

He was standing exactly where I had left him, a cup of tea in his hand. He had been watching. I did not know for how long, but I suspected he had seen more than enough. His face, as ever, was a mask of unreadable calm. He was not scowling. He was not angry. But his grey eyes were fixed on me with a cool, unnerving intensity. It was the look of a man observing a chess piece that had suddenly begun to move in a very unexpected, and very interesting, way. It was the look of a scientist who has noted an anomaly and is now determined to understand its properties.

The look did not condemn. It did not accuse. It simply... saw.

And that was somehow the most terrifying thing of all.

The giddy warmth in my veins turned to ice. The guilt, which had been a quiet hum beneath the surface, now screamed in my ears. I had been caught. Not in the act itself, but in the feeling. He had seen the flush in my cheeks. He had seen the smile I could not hide. He had seen the life that his brother, and not he, had sparked in me.

He knew. And he said nothing.

9

Ink and Intimacy

Araminta

The morning after the Fitzhardings' garden party was quiet. It was a grey, listless sort of day. The weather seemed to be colluding with my conscience, both insisting on a period of somber reflection. I sat in my private sitting room, a book of dry sermons open in my lap. I had read the same page four times. The words refused to arrange themselves into any coherent meaning. My mind was still on a sun-drenched lawn, caught in the unnerving grey gaze of my fiancé.

The Duke's stare had been a silent accusation. He had seen. He had noted my smiles, my laughter, my animation in his brother's presence. He had filed it away in the cold, orderly archives of his mind. And he had said nothing. The not-knowing was a special kind of torment. I was a prisoner awaiting a verdict from a judge who would not speak. It was far worse than a direct confrontation. It was a war of nerves, and I was painfully outmatched.

My lady's maid, Eliza, moved about the room, her movements quiet and efficient. She straightened the drapery. She plumped a cushion. Her presence was usually a comfort, but today it felt like an intrusion on my private misery.

"Will there be anything else, my lady?" she asked, her voice carefully neutral. She was far too perceptive. She knew my moods better than my own mother did.

"No, thank you, Eliza," I said, not looking up from the nonsensical page. "I believe I shall simply read for a while."

It was a lie. I had no intention of reading. I had every intention of sitting here and tormenting myself with replays of every stolen glance, every whispered word.

Just as Eliza reached the door, another servant appeared. He was one of our household footmen, and he looked flustered. He announced, "A messenger for Lady Araminta."

Behind him stood a young boy. He could not have been more than seventeen. He wore the smart, dark green livery of the Greycourt household. He clutched a single, folded letter in his white-gloved hand as if it were a priceless artifact he was terrified of dropping.

My heart gave a single, violent thud against my ribs. It was not a delivery from the Duke. The Duke's correspondence arrived in a formal ducal carriage, delivered by a secretary who looked as old and stern as a gargoyle. This was something else. This was clandestine.

The boy stepped forward, his eyes fixed on the floor. "My lady," he mumbled. "From Lord Evander. I was instructed to deliver it into your hands only."

I could feel Eliza's gaze on me, sharp and questioning. My own hand trembled slightly as I reached out and took the letter. The paper was thick and creamy. It was sealed not with the official Greycourt crest, but with a simple, anonymous wax seal bearing the impression of a chess piece. A knight.

"Thank you," I managed, my voice a dry whisper. "There is no reply."

The boy bowed hastily and practically scurried from the room, our footman giving me one last curious look before following. The door clicked shut, leaving me alone with Eliza. And the letter.

"Lord Evander?" Eliza's voice was quiet, but it held the weight of a dozen questions.

"A follow-up from the croquet match, I imagine," I said, attempting a casual, dismissive tone. It was a dreadful failure. My cheeks were on fire. "Some foolish wager we made."

"I see, my lady." Her voice told me she did not see at all. She saw a secret.

She saw a danger. She hesitated for a moment, as if wanting to say more. But she was a good servant. She held her tongue. With one last, worried glance, she curtseyed and left me in silence.

The moment the door was closed, I sank into a chair, my legs suddenly weak. The letter felt warm in my hand. It was a dangerous object. It was a spark in a room filled with dry tinder. I should burn it. I should throw it into the fire without a second thought. It was the only sensible, honorable thing to do.

My fingers broke the seal.

I unfolded the single sheet of paper. The handwriting was just as I had imagined it would be. It was a bold, energetic scrawl that slanted across the page with a confidence that bordered on arrogance. It was the complete opposite of the Duke's neat, controlled script.

My eyes devoured the words.

```
My Dearest Lady Araminta,
I must formally lodge a complaint. Your performance at croquet
yesterday has left me in a state of deep distress. Not your
playing, which was of a delightfully abysmal quality, but your
presence. You have made all future garden parties an impossible
prospect. They will now seem unbearably dull in comparison. It is
a cruel and unusual punishment, and I demand satisfaction.
I have spent the morning attempting to capture the tragic spirit
of our game. I believe you will find the attached sketch to be a
work of heartbreaking realism.
```

My gaze fell to the bottom of the page. There, he had sketched a tiny, comical drawing. It was a croquet mallet, but he had given it arms and legs. It was weeping dramatically over a ball that had a distinctly stubborn and uncooperative expression on its face. Beside the sketch was a tiny, winking eye.

A laugh burst out of me. It was a sudden, genuine, out-loud laugh that echoed in the quiet room. It was a sound of pure, unadulterated delight. The man was impossible. He was outrageous. He was corresponding with his brother's fiancée and including cheeky illustrations.

My heart did a dizzying flip-flop in my chest. This note, this single sheet of paper, held more life and humor and personality than every conversation I had ever had with Thaddeus combined. I read it again, savoring every word, my cheeks warm, my spirit soaring.

This was madness. It was glorious, wonderful madness.

And I knew, with a certainty that defied all logic and propriety, that I had to write back.

I went to my writing desk. I took out a sheet of my finest cream-colored paper. I dipped my pen in the inkwell. This was it. This was the line. I was about to step over it with my eyes wide open.

My pen hovered over the page. What could I say? How could I match his wit? How could I be playful without being improper? My mind, usually so quick with a retort, was a complete blank.

I was so consumed, so focused on the blank page before me, that I did not hear the footsteps in the hallway.

"Araminta?"

My mother's voice from just outside the door was like a pistol shot.

Panic, cold and absolute, seized me. My eyes flew to the letter on my desk. Evander's letter. With its incriminating sketch and its familiar scrawl. It lay there in plain sight, a confession in ink.

The doorknob turned.

I had no time to think. My hand shot out. I snatched the letter. I shoved it frantically under a heavy volume of poetry that lay on the corner of my desk. The book, *Sonnets of the Great Masters*, was a gift from a great-aunt. It was notoriously dense and dull. No one in this house would ever dream of opening it.

The door swung open. My mother, Beatrice Wexley, sailed into the room, a whirlwind of lavender silk and purpose. I sat frozen at my desk, my heart hammering against my ribs so hard I was sure she could see the frantic pulse in my throat. I prayed my face was not as flushed as it felt.

"There you are, dear," she said, her eyes sweeping the room before landing on me. "I was just speaking with Madame Lisette. She can accommodate a fitting for your wedding gown this Thursday. I told her we would be there at two."

My wedding gown. The words were a cruel irony. I was sitting here, hiding a secret letter from another man, while my mother discussed the stitching on the gown I would wear to marry his brother.

"Thursday at two," I repeated, my voice sounding strained and foreign. "Yes, that is fine, Mama."

"Good." She drifted closer to the desk, and my entire body went rigid. Her gaze fell upon the blank sheet of paper and the inkwell. "Writing letters?"

"Just a note to my cousin Theodosia," I lied, the name popping into my head from nowhere. "To thank her for the birthday felicitations."

"How thoughtful of you." My mother trailed a finger along the spine of the book under which the letter was hidden. *Sonnets of the Great Masters.* My heart stopped. For one terrifying second, I was convinced she would pick it up. That she would ask me about my sudden interest in sixteenth-century poetry. That Evander's letter would flutter out onto the floor.

But she did not. Her mind was on other, more important matters. "I do think we should insist on Brussels lace for the sleeves, not Alençon. It has a much finer appearance. It is what a duchess should wear. We must project the proper image from the very start."

"Of course, Mama," I managed to choke out.

She smiled, satisfied. "Very good. Well, do not let me interrupt your correspondence." She turned and, with a rustle of silk, swept out of the room, closing the door behind her.

I did not move for a full minute. I sat perfectly still, my hand resting on the heavy book, my breath coming in short, ragged gasps. The adrenaline was a wild, metallic taste in my mouth. I felt weak with relief, my limbs trembling.

The near discovery had changed everything. It had sent a jolt of pure, undiluted reality through me. This was not a game. This was not a harmless flirtation. This was a secret. A real, tangible, and deeply dangerous secret that could, in an instant, bring my entire world crashing down.

And the terror of that realization was matched only by the thrilling, undeniable surge of life it sent through my veins.

My resolve, which had been wavering, now hardened into steel. I pulled the book away. I retrieved Evander's letter, my fingers tracing his signature. The danger had not scared me off. It had made me bolder.

I took up my pen again. My hand was steady now. The words came easily. My own wit, my own spirit, so long suppressed, poured out onto the page.

Lord Evander, I wrote.

```
Your complaint is noted, though I must reject it on the grounds
that any improvement to the Fitzhardings' party was entirely
unintentional. My croquet performance was, I assure you, an act of
genuine ineptitude, not entertainment.
As for your sketch, while your artistic talents are clearly
formidable, I fear you have misjudged the mallet. It was not
weeping. It was, in fact, laughing at me. The ball, however, you
have captured perfectly. A more sullen and disagreeable sphere of
painted wood I have never had the displeasure of meeting.
I accept your surrender, but I offer no penance. The memory of
your waistcoat's tragic demise will surely be punishment enough.
Yours in sport,
Lady Araminta Wexley
```

I read it over. It was daring. It was teasing. It was me. A version of me I had almost forgotten existed.

I folded the paper with deliberate care. I found my own sealing wax and a small signet with my initial, A. I lit the candle, my hand not shaking in the slightest now. I melted the dark blue wax, the flame dancing in my eyes. I pressed the seal firmly onto the folded paper.

The act was final. It was a commitment. I had not just written a letter. I had cast my lot.

I held the sealed reply in my hand, a small, dangerous piece of my own soul. My heart was a frantic drum in my chest. It was a rhythm of pure, unadulterated joy. And it was a rhythm of profound, terrifying fear. I had entered into a secret correspondence with my fiancé's brother. I was venturing into the deepest, most treacherous waters imaginable.

And I had absolutely no desire to turn back.

10

Close Quarters

Araminta

Circumstances, I was learning, had a wicked sense of humor. The universe seemed determined to throw me into Lord Evander Greycourt's path with the enthusiasm of a new matchmaker. And I, with my pathetic, traitorous heart, seemed equally determined to stumble directly into him.

The latest test of my non-existent resolve was a weekend party at Albrey Park, the country estate of Lord and Lady Albrey. It was a sprawling, handsome house set in the middle of a thousand acres of aggressively green parkland. We were there, ostensibly, to enjoy the country air. In reality, we were there to engage in the same gossip and social maneuvering we did in London, but with the added inconvenience of mud.

I was sitting in the overwarm drawing room, pretending to admire Lady Albrey's needlepoint—a rather lumpy depiction of a sheep that looked profoundly unhappy with its situation—when the Duke approached me. This, in itself, was an event so rare it startled me. He moved with his usual quiet purpose, securing a cup of tea from a passing footman before taking a seat in the chair opposite mine. The heavy silence of the room seemed to bend around him, growing denser. He sat for a moment, contemplating his teacup as if it held state secrets. Then he looked at me.

"Lady Araminta," he began, his voice a low, formal rumble that did little to warm the air between us. "I trust you are finding the country air agreeable?"

It was a stiff, awkward opening, like a line rehearsed from a book on social etiquette. But it was an opening. It was an effort. And it was directed at me. My heart gave a surprised flutter.

"It is a welcome change from London, Your Grace," I replied, my own voice carefully neutral, my posture ramrod straight.

"Indeed." He took a sip of his tea. His eyes scanned my face as if searching for something—a crack in my composure, perhaps. "Lord Albrey mentioned his wife has recently acquired a new pianoforte from Broadwood and Sons. I know you play."

I was stunned into silence. He had remembered. A piece of information about me, something beyond my name and my family's debts, something personal and frivolous, had lodged in his orderly mind. He knew I played the pianoforte. The knowledge was so unexpected it felt like a shift in the very foundations of my understanding of him.

"I do, Your Grace," I finally managed, my voice a little breathless. "Though I am sadly out of practice."

"Perhaps you might be persuaded to play for the company after dinner," he suggested. It was not a command. It was, for him, something shockingly close to a request. He was attempting to build a bridge across the vast, silent chasm between us. He was trying to make this engagement work.

The thought was so confounding that I did not know how to respond. A part of me, the dutiful part I had been clinging to for weeks, was pleased. This was good. This was progress. But another, more honest part, felt a wave of profound exhaustion. This was the best he could offer. A stilted, formal conversation about my predictable, lady-like accomplishments. It was the effort of a man attempting to assemble a complex machine, following a set of instructions, not one trying to connect with a person. The bridge he was building was cold and made of stone; it was not a structure meant for warmth.

Before I could formulate a reply that was both polite and noncommittal, our host, Lord Albrey, descended upon us, his face alight with agricultural fervor.

"Renshawe!" he boomed, his voice echoing in the crowded room. "A moment, if you please. My man has just reported an issue with the new drainage system in the north field. I would value your opinion immensely."

The Duke's entire demeanor shifted. The vague, dutiful attention he had been directing at me sharpened into a look of keen, focused interest. He turned his body, a subtle but complete pivot, away from me and toward Lord Albrey. The fragile, awkward bridge he had been building between us crumbled into dust.

"The clay content of the soil in that particular quadrant is problematic," Thaddeus said, his voice alive with an energy I had never once heard directed at me. "Did you increase the gradient by the percentage I suggested?"

They were instantly lost, their conversation a dense forest of gradients and soil composition and drainage tiles. Thaddeus had looked more animated talking about manure than he had ever looked talking to me. I was once again invisible, an ornamental accessory to a conversation that did not concern me. And the brief, stilted effort he had made only made the subsequent dismissal feel that much sharper, that much more profound.

It was then I felt the desperate need to escape. The drawing room was overwarm and smelled of damp wool and old grudges. I slipped out onto a stone terrace overlooking the west lawn. The air was cool and heavy with the promise of rain. Dark, bruised-looking clouds were gathering on the horizon with alarming speed. A restless wind whipped at the hem of my walking dress. It felt like a reflection of my own internal state. Restless. Unsettled. A storm waiting to break.

The first drop of rain was a cold shock against my cheek. Within seconds, the heavens opened. A sudden, violent downpour began, turning the placid afternoon into a grey, streaming chaos. Guests shrieked and ran for cover. I gathered my skirts and fled toward the nearest entrance, a side door I had noticed earlier. I fumbled with the heavy oak door, pushed it open, and stumbled inside, gasping for breath.

I found myself in a library. It was magnificent, two stories of bookshelves creating canyons of leather-bound spines. The air smelled of old paper, beeswax, and rain. It was blessedly, profoundly quiet. I leaned against the closed door for a moment, my heart pounding from the run, and savored the silence.

The door opened again behind me, so suddenly that I jumped.

"It seems the heavens have declared war," a familiar, laughing voice said.

I turned. Evander stood in the doorway, shaking rain from his dark blue coat. His hair was damp and tousled, falling across his forehead in a way that was entirely too appealing. He grinned.

"My goodness, Lady Araminta," he said, his smile widening as he took in my disheveled state. "You look like a beautiful, half-drowned sea nymph who has just washed ashore. I confess, I am tempted not to offer you a towel, as the effect is remarkably fetching."

"And you, my lord, look as though you have been swimming in the ornamental lake," I retorted, a smile tugging at my own lips despite my best efforts to remain stern.

He laughed, a rich, warm sound that filled the quiet space. But just as he stepped further in, the door opened again. And again. A torrent of damp, chattering guests poured in. The quiet sanctuary was instantly transformed into a crowded, noisy drawing room, filled with complaints about the weather and laments over ruined attire.

"So much for a quiet refuge," Evander murmured, his voice close to my ear. He gestured with his head toward a narrow, shadowed space between two towering bookshelves at the far end of the room. "A tactical retreat is in order, I think. Shall we?"

It was a suggestion. It was a conspiracy. I gave a small, almost imperceptible nod.

The alcove was a tiny, forgotten world, a narrow canyon of books. The roar of the rain against the tall library windows was a constant, soothing hum. We stood shoulder to shoulder. Our arms brushed. I could feel the heat of his body through the fabric of my dress. I was acutely, agonizingly aware of him. I focused my attention on the books beside me, their titles a meaningless blur of gold leaf on dark leather. *A History of Ecclesiastical Law. Treatises on Ancient Navigation.* I did not read them. I just stared, praying he could not hear the frantic beat of my heart.

"I received your letter," he said, his voice a low, intimate vibration that seemed to travel directly through my bones. "It was witty, and sharp, and I have read it at least five times. I am beginning to think you are a dangerous woman, Lady Araminta."

"I assure you, my lord," I whispered, my eyes still fixed on the unread books, "I am the furthest thing from dangerous."

"Are you?" he murmured. I could feel his gaze on me, warm and intent. "A woman who can wield a pen like a sword? Who can make a man laugh from across a crowded lawn? I find that terrifying. And terribly alluring." He paused, letting the silence stretch. "So, about our rematch. I propose we raise the stakes."

My breath hitched. "Stakes, my lord?"

"Indeed. A simple wager is so uninspired. I propose this: the loser of our next match must confess a secret. A real one. Something they have never told another living soul."

The challenge hung in the air, audacious and thrilling. This was not a game of croquet he was proposing. It was a game of intimacy. A game of souls.

"I think not, my lord," I said, my voice betraying me with a slight tremor. "I have no secrets to confess."

"Oh, I think you do," he said softly, his voice a seductive caress. "I think you are full of secrets. I should very much like to be the one you tell them to."

His words were a soft caress, wrapping around me, warm and intoxicating. I risked a glance at him then. His face was close. His hazel eyes were dark and serious in the dim light, the playful humor gone, replaced by an intensity that made my breath catch.

I knew I should move. I shifted my weight, a small, preparatory movement to step away. My foot, clad in its ruined, damp slipper, came down on an uneven spot on the floor. A loose floorboard.

My ankle turned. I was thrown off balance, a small gasp escaping my lips as I pitched forward.

Instantly, his arm shot out, wrapping around my waist like a steel band, hauling me back against him. The world stopped.

One moment, I was stumbling. The next, I was flush against the solid length of his body. My hands were pressed flat against his chest. I could feel the steady, strong beat of his heart beneath my palm. It was a rhythm utterly at odds with the frantic, panicked fluttering of my own. His arm was a circle of heat at my waist, holding me fast. His breath was warm against my hair.

"Araminta," he breathed, his voice a raw, shaken whisper, a sound of pure possession.

I should have pushed away. I should have been horrified. But my body, that great traitor, betrayed me. It melted against him. It recognized something in his hold, in his solid presence, that felt less like a scandal and more like a homecoming.

He did not release me. His arm remained firmly around my waist. His other hand came up to rest lightly on my arm, a gesture of reassurance that felt anything but reassuring. It felt like a brand. I tilted my head back to look up at him. His expression was taut, his jaw tight. His dark eyes searched mine, and I saw a reflection of my own turmoil there. A war between duty and desire.

The urge to rise on my toes, to close the small, agonizing distance between our lips, was a physical force, a craving so intense it was a painful ache in my chest. I saw his gaze drop to my mouth. His breath hitched.

A woman's shrill laugh echoed from the main part of the library, loud and jarring. It was followed by the sound of approaching footsteps.

The spell shattered.

We sprang apart as if burned. The sudden cold where his body had been was a physical shock. I stumbled back against the bookshelves, my face flaming, my entire body trembling. Evander took a half-step back, running a shaky hand through his hair. He would not meet my eyes.

The footsteps grew closer. Two of Lord Albrey's guests ambled past the mouth of our alcove, arguing about a misplaced card case. They did not even glance in our direction. They were gone as quickly as they had appeared.

But the moment was gone with them. The charged, private world we had occupied for a few heart-stopping seconds had been irrevocably breached. We were no longer two people alone in the shadows. We were Lady Araminta Wexley, betrothed to a duke, and Lord Evander Greycourt, his brother. And we had just come dangerously close to committing an unforgivable sin.

"I..." I started, my voice a broken whisper. I could not finish.

"Araminta," he breathed again, his voice raw with a thousand unspoken things.

"I must go," I said quickly. I could not look at him. I could not bear to see the regret that I knew must be in his eyes.

Before he could say another word, I fled. I pushed past him out of the alcove, my head down, and hurried through the crowded library. I did not stop until I was back in the hallway, my hand pressed against my racing heart.

My longing, which had been a secret, simmering thing, was now a raging, undeniable fire. The damage was done. We had not kissed. We had not even spoken of what we felt. But he had held me. And in that one, brief, accidental embrace, a line had been crossed. And I knew, with a chilling certainty, that I could never go back.

11

The Ghost of a Touch

Araminta

I fled. I did not look back. The crowded library was a blur of startled faces and bright colors. I moved through them like a phantom, my only thought to escape, to find a door, to find a quiet space where I could fall apart in private. My heart hammered against my ribs, a wild, panicked drumbeat against the cage of my own making.

I found my assigned room. I shut the door behind me, leaning against the solid oak as if to bolt it against the world. Against him. Against myself. I was trembling from head to toe. My gown was still damp from the rain. My hair was a wild mess. My hands were shaking so violently I could not clasp them together.

I was a ruin. A complete and utter ruin.

Eliza was not there, thank God. I could not have borne her quiet, knowing eyes. I could not have borne her gentle questions. I needed to be alone with this catastrophe, this glorious, terrible, world-ending thing that had happened in the library.

I paced the floor of the room, a caged animal in a silk dress. I walked from the window to the fireplace, from the bed to the door, my footsteps a frantic, restless rhythm on the polished floorboards. But there was no escape. The memory was not in the library. It was in me. It was seared onto my skin.

His arm.

The thought was a physical jolt. I stopped in the center of the room, my hand flying to my waist, to the very spot where his arm had wrapped around me. I could still feel it. A phantom pressure. A circle of heat. A brand of impossible intimacy.

My mind, against my will, replayed the moment with a torturous, perfect clarity. The stumble. The gasp. The world tilting on its axis. And then the sudden, shocking solidity of him. He had not just caught me. He had hauled me back against him, his arm a steel band, his body a shield. It was not a polite, hesitant steadying. It was a raw, masculine reflex. An instinct. *Mine. Safe.*

I closed my eyes, and I was there again. I could feel the hard, unyielding wall of his chest against my palms. I could feel the steady, powerful beat of his heart under my hand, a rhythm so calm and sure, so utterly at odds with the frantic terror of my own. I could smell the clean, sharp scent of the rain on his coat, mingled with the warm, spicy fragrance of sandalwood that was purely him. It was the scent of a man who lived and breathed and walked in the sun and the rain. It was the scent of life itself.

And his voice. He had whispered my name. *Araminta.* Not Lady Araminta. Not a title or a formality. Just my name, breathed against my hair, a raw, shaken sound of possession.

A sob, sharp and painful, escaped my throat. This was the true nature of my ruin. It was not just that I had been indiscreet. It was not just that I had been caught in a scandalous position with my fiancé's brother. It was that in that one, brief, accidental moment, I had felt something I had never known existed.

Safety. Desire. A sense of belonging so profound it shook me to my very soul.

My mind, a cruel prosecutor, presented its next piece of evidence. It conjured the image of Thaddeus. It replayed every touch I had ever received from him.

I remembered the day of our betrothal. He had taken my hand to place the ring on my finger. His grip was light, correct, and utterly devoid of warmth. He had held my hand as if it were a fragile, priceless porcelain object he was afraid of breaking, an asset he was carefully cataloging.

I remembered the countless balls and soirees. His hand would rest on the small of my back, a cool, proprietary weight. It was not a caress. It was a signal to the world. *This one belongs to me.* His touch was a gesture of ownership, not intimacy. It was the touch of a man guiding a prized mare, not holding a woman.

I recalled our stilted conversation just this afternoon. His awkward attempt at connection. Even then, there had been a vast, unbridgeable distance between us. He had looked at me, yes, but it was with the scrutiny of a man assessing a balance sheet. He was checking on his investment.

Thaddeus had touched me, but he had never truly *held* me. He had never surrounded me with his strength, never made me feel as if the world could fall away and he would be the one solid thing left standing.

Until Evander.

The comparison was a brutal, physical pain. It was a grief for a warmth I had never known I was lacking. The careful, orderly world I had constructed for myself, the one where I would trade passion for security, where I would be a good, dutiful duchess, it all seemed like a foolish, childish fantasy. A lie I had told myself to make the cage seem more palatable.

The guilt came next, a sickening, churning wave. I was promised to another man. A good man, in his own way. A man who was saving my family. And I was standing in my room, obsessing over the touch of his brother. I was replaying the memory of that embrace with a longing so intense it was a physical ache. It was a betrayal of the highest order. It was a sin.

But the longing would not be denied. It was a fire now, a steady, burning flame that had been fanned from a simple spark. I had been attracted to Evander's wit, to his laughter, to the life in his eyes. But now, it was more. So much more.

I now craved the feeling of his arm around my waist. I craved the steady beat of his heart against my hand. I craved the safety and the danger and the sheer, unadulterated life I had felt in his arms. It was a hunger I had never known. And he had awakened it with a single, reflexive touch.

I moved to the window and stared out at the storm. The rain lashed against the glass, the wind howled, a perfect reflection of the tempest inside me. The world outside was a grey, streaming chaos. I felt a kinship with it.

I wrapped my arms around myself, a poor substitute for the hold I truly wanted. My fingers traced the spot on my waist where his arm had been. The ghost of a touch. It was all I had. A memory. But it was more real, more potent, than any physical reality I had with the Duke.

My feelings for Evander Greycourt had solidified. They had moved beyond a dangerous flirtation, beyond a secret correspondence. They had become a deep, desperate, and terrifying yearning. I was no longer a woman entertaining a harmless fancy. I was a woman who had been shown what it felt like to be truly held, and who now knew, with a certainty that was both a curse and a blessing, that she could never, ever settle for anything less again.

I lay awake for hours that night, long after the storm outside had passed. The house was silent. The world was still. But in the darkness of my room, my heart raged on, haunted by the memory of a stolen moment in a library, and the ghost of a touch that had ruined me forever.

12

The Point of No Return

Evander

The mask I wore in public was that of a charming, carefree rogue. It was a well-crafted, comfortable thing. It allowed me to move through the world with an easy grace, to charm and to tease, to take nothing seriously. It was a lie, of course. But it was a useful lie.

Tonight, in the solitude of my rooms at Albrey Park, the mask was gone. And the man underneath was a stranger to me. He was agitated. He was tormented. He was a man on fire.

I paced the floor, the rhythmic thud of my boots on the old oak boards doing nothing to quiet the storm in my head. The rain still lashed against the windowpanes, a wild, relentless drumming that echoed the frantic beat of my own heart. I went to the small table where a decanter of brandy sat, a rich, amber promise of oblivion. I poured a generous measure, my hand shaking slightly. I tossed it back in one go, the fiery liquid burning a path down my throat.

It did nothing. The brandy was a weak, pathetic thing against the raging inferno of my thoughts. The fire had a name.

Araminta.

I closed my eyes, and I was back in that damned library. In that perfect,

58

cursed alcove. I saw it all with a clarity that was a form of exquisite torture. The way she had looked up at me, her eyes wide and startled. The slight tremor in her voice. The way she had stumbled.

And the way I had caught her.

It had been an instinct. Pure, unthinking reflex. My arm had shot out, my hand closing around her waist, hauling her back against me before my mind had even registered the danger. The feeling of her in my arms... Christ. It was a revelation. I had expected her to be a fragile, bird-like thing. But she was not. She was slender, yes, but she was solid. Real. A warm, living woman pressed against me. Her hands had landed on my chest, and I had felt the slight, shocked pressure of her fingertips through the wool of my coat.

My mind, a cruel and relentless artist, began to paint the details I had missed in the chaos. The scent of her. It was not the simple lavender or rosewater of other ladies. It was something more complex. The clean, sharp smell of the rain in her hair. The faint, warm fragrance of her skin. The subtle, sweet scent that was purely, intoxicatingly her. It was a scent I knew would now haunt my dreams.

I groaned, turning away from the window. This was madness. This was a path to ruin. She was my brother's betrothed. The future Duchess of Renshawe. She was duty and honor and family alliances. She was everything I was not supposed to want.

And I had never wanted anything more in my entire life.

I poured another brandy. This time, I drank it slowly, letting the fire burn. But it could not burn away the memory. It could not burn away the fantasy that was now taking root in my mind. The fantasy of what *should* have happened next.

In my mind, the footsteps in the library never came. The shrill laugh never shattered the spell. We were still there, in that secret world of shadows and books, her body pressed against mine, my arm a possessive circle around her.

In this fantasy, I did not let her go.

My other hand comes up, not to steady her arm, but to cup her jaw. My thumb strokes the soft, delicate line of her cheek, feeling the frantic pulse that beats there. She does not pull away. Her eyes, wide and dark in the dim light, are full of a terrified, breathtaking wanting. She is as lost in this as I am.

"Araminta," I whisper, my voice a raw, husky thing.

And then I kiss her.

It is not a gentle kiss. It is not a polite, hesitant exploration. It is a claiming. It is the kiss of a man who has been starved and has just been offered a feast. It is all the witty remarks, all the stolen glances, all the secret letters, finally given a voice, a body. My mouth covers hers, and it is a clash of desperation and desire. She tastes of lemonade and rain and a sweet, intoxicating innocence that I am about to ruin. She makes a small sound in the back of her throat, a soft, broken sigh of surrender that sets my blood on fire. Her hands, which were pressed flat against my chest, now fist in the fabric of my coat, holding on as if she is drowning and I am the only solid thing in her world.

I shook my head and tried to erase those dirty thoughts, but it becomes more dangerous. More possessive. My lips leave hers, a reluctant parting. But I am not done with her. My mouth trails a path of fire along her jawline, to the delicate, sensitive spot just below her ear. I feel the frantic beat of her pulse against my lips. Thump-thump. Thump-thump. It is the sound of her life, and I want to consume it. I press a kiss to that spot, a deliberate, marking kiss. This is not the charming rake now. This is a man. A man who wants to possess, to own.

I breathe in her scent, and I imagine whispering against her skin, *'Mine. You are mine, not his. Mine.'*

I imagined the feel of her fingers tangling in my hair, pulling me closer. I imagined the way she would arch into me, her body a perfect, pliant fit against mine. I imagined...

I slammed the empty brandy glass down on the table with a crack. The sound shattered the sensual, dangerous fantasy. I stood in the center of the room, my breathing ragged, my body taut with a desire so fierce it was a physical pain.

What in God's name was wrong with me?

This was not a game. This was not a flirtation. A man does not imagine possessing a woman's soul over a simple flirtation. A man does not feel this fierce, primal, protective rage at the thought of another man touching her—

even if that man is his own brother.

The moment she had stumbled, the way my arm had shot out to protect her... it had not been just reflex. It had been an instinct buried so deep I had not known it was there. An instinct to shield her. To keep her safe. To keep her for myself.

And her letters. I had kept them all, tucked away in my travel case. I had read them so many times the paper was soft and worn at the creases. I had memorized her wit, the elegant curve of her handwriting. I had found myself looking for her in every room, my day not truly beginning until I had caught a glimpse of her.

My mind, so accustomed to witty deflections and charming evasions, could no longer outrun the truth. It was a simple, stark, and catastrophic truth.

It had only one name.

I sank into a chair, my head in my hands. I said the words aloud, a harsh, broken whisper in the silent, storm-tossed room.

"I am in love with her."

The confession brought no relief. It brought only a profound, crushing sense of doom. The words hung in the air, an admission of treason.

"I am in love with my brother's fiancée."

The full, catastrophic nature of the situation descended upon me. This was not a matter of a brief scandal that could be weathered. This was not a secret affair that could be managed with discretion. This was love. A real, life-altering, soul-deep love for the one woman in the entire world I could not have.

The stakes were no longer just my reputation or her honor. The stakes were now our hearts. Our lives. Our futures. And every possible path forward led to ruin. If I pursued her, I would destroy her. I would tear her from her family's salvation, brand her with a scandal she could never escape, and make her an outcast. I would betray my own brother in the most fundamental way imaginable.

And if I let her go? If I let her marry Thaddeus? The thought was a physical torment. To imagine her in my brother's house, in his life, in his bed... it was a vision of a cold, grey hell. To know that the vibrant, laughing, witty woman I had discovered would be slowly, inevitably extinguished by his cold, dutiful world was an agony.

I felt trapped. Utterly, completely trapped between my newfound love and my unwavering duty. Honor, a concept I had always treated with a certain lighthearted disdain, now felt like a lead weight in my gut.

I was Evander Greycourt. The second son. The charming rogue. My role was to be entertaining, not to fall in love. Especially not with her.

I stood and walked to the window, staring out at the relentless, weeping rain. The love I felt for Araminta was not a gentle, warming flame. It was a wildfire. And I knew, with a certainty that settled in my bones like a deep, unshakable chill, that it was going to burn us all to the ground.

13

A Golden Gilded Cage

Araminta

D uty is a garment one wears. For three days, I had worn mine dutifully. I had buttoned it up to my chin and refused to acknowledge the wild, frantic beating of my heart beneath the fabric. I had returned from Albrey Park and locked the memory of the library away in a dark, cold corner of my mind. The ghost of Evander's touch, the scent of his coat, the raw want in his eyes—I had banished them all. I was Lady Araminta Wexley. I was to be the Duchess of Renshawe. I would perform my part.

Tonight's performance was to be at a formal dinner party hosted by Lord Grenville, a man whose political influence was matched only by the profound dullness of his conversation. The dining room was a formidable space. Dark wood paneling, a veritable army of silver cutlery, and a centerpiece so large it obscured one's view of the person sitting opposite. The atmosphere was rigid, stuffy, and suffocatingly important. It was Thaddeus's natural habitat.

I sat to his right, a perfect model of ducal propriety. I smiled. I made polite, meaningless conversation with the gentleman to my other side, a Sir Reginald Croft, whose primary topic of interest was his own gout. I was playing my role to perfection. I was a statue. A lovely, well-dressed, and entirely lifeless statue. I told myself this was enough. This was my life now.

And then, I made a mistake.

Sir Reginald, having exhausted the topic of his swollen joints, turned to the lady on his other side. I was left in a brief, blessed moment of silence. The gentleman on my left, a younger man named Mr. Alcott with kind eyes and an enthusiastic demeanor, leaned toward me.

"Forgive my interruption, Lady Araminta," he said, his voice a pleasant, low tenor. "But I overheard you mention your travels in Italy some years ago. Did you by any chance visit the Uffizi Gallery in Florence?"

The question was a key, unlocking a room in my mind I had long kept shuttered. Before my father's debts, before my life became a series of transactions, we had spent a glorious summer in Italy.

"I did, Mr. Alcott," I said, and to my own surprise, a genuine smile touched my lips. "It was the most magnificent place I have ever seen."

"Botticelli's *Primavera*," he said, his own face lighting up. "To see it in person... it is not a painting. It is a living thing. The detail in the flowers, the expression on the faces. It is music made visible."

"Yes!" The word escaped me, brighter and more forceful than I had intended. "That is it exactly. Music made visible. And his *Birth of Venus*. The way she seems to float on the air, so ethereal. I remember standing before it for nearly an hour. I could not bring myself to move."

For five minutes, we spoke of art. We spoke of Florence, of the Ponte Vecchio, of the light on the Arno river. We spoke of things that were beautiful and passionate and real. And for five minutes, I forgot where I was. I forgot the stuffy dining room. I forgot the cold diamond on my finger. I forgot the man sitting beside me. I leaned forward, my hands gesturing as I described the sheer, breathtaking beauty of a Raphael Madonna. My face was animated. I was laughing. I was alive.

It was a brief, beautiful lapse. And it was a fatal error.

I felt it before I saw it. A sudden drop in the temperature of the air beside me. A cold, heavy presence that made the hairs on my arms stand up.

Thaddeus.

I trailed off mid-sentence, the joyful memory dissolving like smoke. I turned my head slowly. He had been observing me. His own conversation had ceased.

He was looking at me, his grey eyes as flat and cold as slate. He had watched my entire, animated performance.

He waited for a lull in the table's general conversation, a moment when no one was paying us any mind. Then, he leaned toward me. He did not raise his voice. It was a low, cold murmur that no one else could possibly hear. It was for me alone.

"Araminta."

The sound of my name on his lips was a shard of ice.

"A duchess does not display such unbridled enthusiasm," he said, his voice quiet, precise, and utterly devastating. "She is a model of restraint. Of composure. You would do well to remember that."

He leaned back, picked up his wine glass, and took a slow, deliberate sip. The assassination was complete. It had been executed with his signature quiet, chilling efficiency.

Every drop of warmth, every bit of life, drained out of me. I sat there, my back ramrod straight, my face a frozen, polite mask. But beneath the surface, a cold, hard fury was beginning to form.

This was not just his coldness. This was not his indifference. This was an active attempt to extinguish my spirit. To trim away the parts of me that did not fit his perfect, passionless model of a duchess. He had seen a flicker of my true self, a moment of genuine joy, and his instinct had not been to share it, or even to ignore it, but to snuff it out. It was a deliberate act of erasure.

The memory of Evander rose in my mind, so powerful, so painful, it was like a physical blow. Evander, who had celebrated my wit. Evander, who had called my laugh a miracle. Evander, who had looked at me as if I were a treasure to be discovered, not a statue to be polished. He had wanted to hear my secrets. Thaddeus wanted to silence my opinions.

The contrast was a brutal, clarifying agony.

I endured the rest of the dinner in a state of suspended animation. The food tasted like ash in my mouth. The conversation around me was a meaningless buzz. I smiled. I nodded. I was a perfect automaton. But inside, I was raging. The gilded cage had never felt so small, its bars so cold and hard. And for the first time, I felt the desperate, primal urge to break them.

65

The carriage ride home was silent. But it was my silence now, not just his. It was a cold, hard wall I built around myself, a fortress he could not breach. He had demanded restraint. I would give him restraint. I would give him a silence so profound, so complete, he would feel as though he were sitting beside a ghost.

When we returned home, I did not wait for Eliza. I went straight to my room and closed the door. There were no tears this time. The time for weeping was over. My despair had been burned away by the cold fire of my anger, and what was left was a hard, sharp, and desperate resolve.

I stood in the center of my room, my hands clenched into fists at my sides. I replayed his words. *A model of restraint.* He wanted a possession, not a partner. He wanted a reflection of his own power and control, not a living, breathing woman.

I could not do it. I would not let him erase me. I would rather be ruined than be rendered into nothing.

My feelings for Evander, which I had tried so desperately to suppress, now felt like the only real, true thing left in my life. They were no longer just a source of guilt. They were my only hope. They were the proof that another life was possible, a life where I could be myself, where my spirit was not a flaw to be corrected, but a thing to be cherished.

I had to know. I had to know if what I had felt in his arms was real. I had to know if the man who had looked at me with such warmth and wanting was a fantasy, or if he was a truth I could cling to in this shipwreck of a life. It was no longer a question of romance. It was a question of survival.

I moved to my writing desk, my steps sure and certain. My earlier indecision was gone, replaced by a clarity so fierce it was almost painful. My hand did not shake as I picked up the pen.

The note I wrote was simple. It was heartfelt. And it was the most dangerous thing I had ever done.

```
Lord Evander,
I must speak with you. It is a matter of some urgency. Will you
```

```
meet me? The gazebo in Green Park. At dusk tomorrow.
Araminta
```

I sealed the note, my heart a steady, determined drum. I was no longer a passive victim in the Duke's cold, quiet war. I was taking control. I was making a move. I was setting a course for a new, unknown, and terrifying shore. And I knew, with every fiber of my being, that I would rather drown in the storm than spend one more day suffocating in this gilded cage.

14

Drawing the Line

Evander

The memory of her was a brand.

I had spent two days trying to burn it from my mind. I drank more brandy than was strictly advisable. I rode my horse into the ground. I even attempted to read a book on political theory my brother had recommended, a punishment of such profound dullness it should have scoured my mind clean of all thought.

Nothing worked.

Every time I closed my eyes, I was back in that library alcove. I felt the slender weight of her as she stumbled against me. I smelled the scent of her hair, that clean, floral fragrance mixed with the smell of rain. I saw the look in her eyes as she tilted her face up to mine. A look of surprise, and fear, and a dawning, undeniable wanting that mirrored my own.

That moment had been a revelation. And a death sentence.

The flirtation, the stolen glances, the secret letters—I had told myself it was a harmless game. I was bringing a little light into the eyes of a woman who was being sold into a life of cold, orderly duty. I was a brief, charming diversion. A pleasant chapter before she began the long, dull book of her life as the Duchess of Renshawe.

I was a fool. A liar.

It was not a game. It had stopped being a game the moment I sketched a weeping croquet mallet and felt a jolt of pure joy imagining her laugh. It had stopped being a game when her witty, intelligent replies became the brightest point of my day. And it had certainly stopped being a game when I held her in my arms and the only thought in my head was *mine*.

She was not mine. She could never be mine.

She belonged to my brother. She belonged to a title, to a dynasty. I was the second son. The charming, reckless Evander with a modest income and a reputation for irresponsibility. What could I offer her? A life of scandal? Ruin? A passionate affair followed by her inevitable disgrace?

I looked at my own reflection in the dark glass of the window. I saw a man who had always taken the easy path. I charmed my way into society, and I charmed my way out of trouble. But there was no charming my way out of this. To continue down this path with her would be the most selfish act of my life. It would destroy her. It would shatter the fragile peace she was trying to make with her fate. It would ruin her family. And it would be an unforgivable betrayal of my brother.

Thaddeus was cold. He was exacting. He was, at times, an impossible man to love. But he was my brother. He was the Duke. And he was offering her a protection, a stability, that I never could.

I had to end it. I had to be the villain. I had to cut out this bright, beautiful thing between us before it grew into a monster that would consume us both.

My hand was steady as I wrote the note. I used my plainest stationery. The words were stark. No witty opening. No charming close. Just a request. An insistence. *Meet me at the gazebo in Green Park at dusk.*

I sent it with a footman and then I waited. The waiting was its own form of torture.

Dusk in the park was a melancholy affair. The sun bled out of the sky, leaving behind streaks of bruised purple and faded orange. The air grew cool. The lamps were not yet lit. It was a world of grey shadows and quiet goodbyes. The setting was appropriate.

I stood in the center of the old stone gazebo, my hands clenched into fists

69

in my pockets. I felt like an executioner awaiting his victim. Every rustle of leaves, every distant laugh, made my nerves jump. What if she did not come? Part of me prayed she would not. It would make this so much easier.

But she did.

I saw her walking along the path, a solitary figure in a simple, elegant gown of pale blue. She moved with a grace that made my chest ache. She looked... hopeful. Questioning. And the sight of that fragile hope on her face was like a physical blow. It made what I was about to do feel infinitely more cruel.

She entered the gazebo, a faint, lovely scent of lavender trailing her. "Evander," she said, her voice soft, a question in that single word. "Is everything alright?"

I could not look at her. I fixed my gaze on a crack in the stone floor. If I looked into her eyes, I would lose my nerve. I knew it.

"No," I said. My voice was a hoarse stranger's. "Nothing is alright, Araminta. We cannot continue this."

I heard her small, sharp intake of breath. The silence that followed was heavy with her confusion. I forced myself to look up.

Her face had fallen. The light, the life I had so enjoyed coaxing out of her, was gone. It was as if I had personally snuffed it out. Her lips were slightly parted in surprise. Her eyes were wide with a dawning hurt that shattered me.

"I... I don't understand," she whispered.

"You do," I said, my voice harder than I intended. I had to be cruel. It was the only way. "You know exactly what I mean. The letters. The croquet game. The library. It all has to stop. Now. Before it is too late."

Her beautiful eyes glistened with unshed tears. My resolve crumbled into dust. My hands ached with the need to reach for her, to smooth the worried line between her brows, to cup her face and tell her the truth. The truth was that I was falling for her. The truth was that the thought of her marrying my brother felt like a physical wound. The truth was that I was a coward.

Instead, I held my ground. I clenched my fists tighter, my nails digging into my palms. The small pain was a grounding thing.

"You're promised to a duke," I said, the words a cold, hard litany of facts. I was reminding myself as much as her. "You are to be the Duchess of Renshawe.

Your family is depending on you. Your future is set." I finally met her gaze, forcing all the feeling from my own. "I am a second son. A flirtation. I am a mistake you cannot afford to make."

A single tear escaped and traced a silent path down her cheek. She did not wipe it away. She just stood there, her chin held high, her devastation a quiet, dignified thing that was a thousand times more painful to witness than any screaming tirade would have been.

"So this was all just a game to you?" she asked, her voice trembling with the effort to keep it steady. "A diversion?"

The lie was a bitter, metallic taste in my mouth. It felt like swallowing broken glass. But it was a necessary lie. It would give her anger. It would give her pride. It would give her a reason to hate me. And hating me was far safer for her than the alternative.

"Yes," I said. The word tore from my throat. "It was a flirtation. A bit of fun. But it has gone too far. It has become... complicated."

"Complicated," she repeated, her voice hollow.

I had to end this. I could not stand here and watch her break because of me.

"For the sake of your future," I said, my voice shaking despite my best efforts. "For your honor. For my brother. We must pretend none of this ever happened. From this day forward, if we should meet, we are nothing more than future relations. Formality. Distance. It is the only way."

I had to leave. Now. If I stayed one second longer, I would destroy us both. I would take her in my arms, and I would never let her go.

So I turned my back on her. I turned my back on the tears glistening on her cheeks, on the silent pain in her eyes, on the one woman who had ever made me feel like more than just a charming rogue.

I walked away. I did not run. I forced myself to walk at a steady, deliberate pace out of the gazebo and down the darkening path. Every step was an act of physical torment. Every instinct screamed at me to turn around, to go back, to tell her the truth.

But I did not look back. I could not.

Because I was doing the first truly honorable thing in my entire life. And it felt exactly like dying.

15

Masquerade of Desire

Araminta

The weeks following my encounter with Evander in the park were a study in grey. My life, which had briefly flared with color, had returned to its natural state of muted obedience. I moved through my days like a ghost in my own body. I smiled when I was expected to smile. I spoke when spoken to. I endured fittings for a wedding gown that felt more like a burial shroud. My heart, which had been so foolishly, painfully alive, had retreated into a numb, aching silence.

Evander's words were a constant, echoing torment. *A mistake you can't afford.* He had dismissed what was between us as a mere flirtation. He had drawn a line of cold, hard duty between us. And I, with my shattered pride, had no choice but to respect it. I had not seen him. I had not heard from him. The silence from him was as profound and absolute as the silence from his brother.

Tonight was the grand summer masquerade at Vauxhall Gardens. It was the most anticipated event of the season, a night of fantasy and disguise, of hidden identities and delicious possibility. For me, it felt like a sentence.

My gown was a confection of silver tissue and moonlight-colored silk. My mask was a delicate, gilded thing that covered the top half of my face, leaving my mouth bare. A mouth that had forgotten the shape of a real smile. The disguise felt less like a liberation and more like a prettier cage. It hid my face, but it could not hide the desolation in my soul.

The Duke arrived to collect me. His costume was simple, severe, and entirely in character. He wore immaculate black evening attire and a plain black silk mask that seemed only to accentuate the cold authority of his jaw. He looked less like a guest at a ball and more like a phantom judge come to preside over the frivolity.

He was silent in the carriage. His silence was a familiar pressure, a weight in the air I had grown accustomed to. But tonight, it felt heavier. Charged.

We arrived at the gardens. They were transformed. Thousands of lanterns hung from the trees, casting a magical, golden glow over the winding paths. Music from a hidden orchestra drifted on the warm night air. The gardens were filled with a swirling, laughing throng of humanity, their faces hidden behind masks of every shape and description. Peacocks and pirates mingled with shepherdesses and sultans. It was a chaotic, beautiful, and utterly unreal world.

I thought, foolishly, that I might be able to lose myself in it. I could fade into the background, a silver ghost among many. I could simply endure the night at a quiet distance.

Thaddeus had other plans.

Before I could take a single step toward the shadows, his hand closed on my arm. His grip was firm, inescapable. He stopped me under the bright glare of a string of lanterns.

"You seem... subdued of late, my dear," he remarked. His voice was a smooth, low murmur, yet it cut through the noise of the party with chilling precision. "I trust you are well?"

My blood ran cold. It was the first personal observation he had made about my state of being since our engagement began. And it was not an expression of concern. It was an interrogation.

"Perfectly well, Your Grace," I lied, my voice tight. "The heat, perhaps."

His eyes, visible through the stark slits of his mask, were unnervingly sharp. They held mine. "Indeed," he said, his tone flat. He paused for a beat, a masterful use of silence. "My brother's company seems to have lost its appeal."

The words were a stiletto, slid cleanly and quietly between my ribs. He knew. He had to know. The dismissal in the park, my subsequent misery—he had observed it all. He had connected the events with his cold logic. He was not an oblivious fiancé. He was a watchful, intelligent adversary. And he was letting me know that he was watching.

"I have not had the pleasure of Lord Evander's company recently," I managed, my voice a credit to years of social training. It did not tremble.

"A loss, I am sure," he said, his voice devoid of any discernible emotion. He released my arm. "Enjoy the gardens, Lady Araminta."

He turned and was immediately swallowed by a group of men that included a government minister and a foreign ambassador. He had delivered his warning. He had asserted his knowledge, his power. And then he had left me, my heart pounding with a fresh, cold fear.

I stood frozen for a moment, the joyous chaos of the masquerade swirling around me. I felt profoundly alone, seen and dissected by the one man I was bound to, yet invisible to everyone else. I pulled my composure around me like a shield and began to walk, my only goal to find a quiet, dark corner where I could simply cease to exist for a few hours.

I was so lost in my own panicked thoughts that I did not notice the figure who had stepped into my path until he spoke.

"May I have this dance, my lady?"

I looked up. He was tall, dressed in a simple but exquisitely tailored coat of deep cobalt blue. His mask was the same shade, unadorned except for a subtle silver trim. It hid his features, but it could not hide his eyes. They were a familiar, warm hazel, and they seemed to look right through my own mask, into the very heart of my loneliness.

My mind screamed a litany of warnings. *No. Walk away. This is madness. Thaddeus is watching.*

But my heart, that battered, foolish thing, whispered a single, desperate word. *Please.*

The orchestra began a new song. A waltz. Sweeping, passionate, and dangerously romantic.

"I..." I hesitated.

He did not press. He simply stood there, his gloved hand outstretched, an island of quiet invitation in the swirling chaos.

My own hand, acting of its own accord, lifted and settled into his.

He led me onto the vast, open-air dance floor. His hand moved to my waist, a firm, warm pressure that sent a shiver down my spine. It felt... familiar. Terribly, wonderfully familiar. We began to move, two masked, anonymous figures joining the river of dancers under the lantern-lit trees.

I did not know for certain. I could only hope. I let him guide me, my feet moving automatically. We did not speak. The music was our only language. He was a superb dancer, confident and strong, leading me through the intricate turns with an easy grace that made me feel weightless.

Then I felt it. A small, subtle pressure from his thumb, stroking the back of my hand where it rested in his. It was not a grand gesture. It was a tiny, secret thing. A playful, intimate gesture.

A gesture of pure, unadulterated Evander.

My breath caught in my throat. It was him. Of course it was him. My heart gave a wild, frantic leap, a panicked bird taking flight in my chest. He had lied. He had said they must be strangers. He had said it was over. And yet, here he was. He had sought me out. He could not stay away.

As if he could feel my shock, my realization, he leaned in close as we spun in a wide circle. His lips brushed the shell of my ear, his voice a low, husky whisper that was meant for me alone.

"I am a fool, Araminta," he breathed, the words a confession against my skin. "Forgive me. I cannot stay away from you."

The world dissolved. All my resolve, all my pride, all my carefully constructed defenses turned to dust. There was no Duke. There was no duty. There was no tomorrow. There was only this moment, this music, and the man holding me in his arms as if he would never let me go.

Our waltz changed. It was no longer a polite series of steps. It became something else. Something desperate. Passionate. I moved closer, my body molding to his. His hand tightened at my waist, pulling me in until there was no space left between us. We were two halves of a whole, moving as one.

The anonymity of our masks, the swirling chaos of the dance floor, it was our shield. It was our liberation. We were hidden in plain sight, free to express all the longing we had been forced to suppress. I looked up into his eyes, and even through the mask, I saw it all. The regret. The desire. The same hopeless, helpless love that was consuming me.

This was intoxication. This was peril. This was the sweetest, most dangerous poison I had ever tasted. Every beat of the music was a beat of my own racing heart. Every turn was a step closer to ruin. I knew Thaddeus was somewhere in this crowd, his cold eyes possibly watching us at this very moment. I knew this single, stolen dance could cost me everything.

And yet, as Evander spun me under the golden glow of the lanterns, his arm a circle of strength around me, I wished for only one thing.

I wished the music would never, ever end.

16

Silent Witness

Araminta

T he music ended. The final, soaring note of the waltz hung in the warm night air for a moment, then vanished. The world rushed back in—the chatter of the crowd, the scrape of chairs, the distant pop of a champagne cork. For a few glorious minutes, there had been only the music and the man holding me. Now, reality returned, a harsh and unwelcome guest.

Evander's arm was still at my waist. His hand still held mine. We stood frozen for a second on the edge of the dance floor, two masked figures caught in the aftermath of a spell.

"I should return," I breathed, the words a lie. I had no desire to return to anything.

"No," he said, his voice a low, urgent murmur. "Not yet."

He did not release me. Instead, his hand tightened on mine, a possessive, determined grip. He began to lead me away from the dance floor, away from the glittering heart of the party. He guided me toward the shadows at the edge of the gardens. I did not resist. My feet followed him as if they were no longer my own. My will had completely deserted me.

We were both still masked. We were both giddy with the recklessness of what we had just done. A shared, secret smile passed between us as we slipped past a boisterous group of men dressed as Roman senators. We were conspirators. Partners in a beautiful, foolish crime.

"Where are we going?" I whispered, my heart a frantic drum against my ribs.

"Somewhere we can breathe," was all he said.

He found it at the far edge of the formal gardens. It was a secluded stone arbor, almost completely hidden by a thick curtain of overgrown ivy. It was a forgotten corner of the world. Inside, a simple stone bench waited, bathed in the silvery light of the moon. The air was thick and sweet with the scent of night-blooming jasmine. It was a secret place, designed for secret things.

We stepped inside. The sounds of the party became a distant, muted hum. Here, in the heart of the arbor, there was only the soft chirping of crickets and the frantic, echoing beat of my own heart. We were alone. Completely, utterly, and devastatingly alone.

He turned to face me. The moonlight filtered through the leaves overhead, dappling his masked face in shifting patterns of silver and shadow. We stood so close I could see the rapid rise and fall of his chest. He was as breathless as I was.

Desire, raw and potent, flowed between us. It was an almost tangible thing, a current in the still air. All the witty banter, all the teasing smiles, had been kindling. The waltz had been the spark. Now, in the silence of this hidden place, the fire was beginning to burn.

With a hand that trembled slightly, he reached up. His fingers, warm and gentle, brushed against my cheek as he found the ribbon of my mask. My breath caught in my throat. This was it. The final pretense was about to be stripped away.

He slowly, deliberately, untied the ribbon. The gilded mask fell away, and I was bare to his gaze. He looked at me, his eyes dark and intense in the moonlight. He looked at me as if he were seeing me for the first toime. As if he were memorizing every line of my face.

"Araminta," he breathed. My name was a prayer on his lips. It was a sound of pure, aching reverence.

Then, his own hands went to his mask. He untied it and let it fall to the stone floor. And he was no longer a masked stranger, a charming phantom from the ball. He was just Evander. His handsome face was taut with an emotion so powerful it stole my breath. It was a maelstrom of longing, and regret, and a desperate, hopeless wanting that mirrored my own.

This was no longer a game. This was no longer a flirtation. This was real. This was everything.

He did not say a word. He did not have to. His eyes said it all.

He leaned in.

And he kissed me.

It was my first kiss. Not the chaste, dry peck on the cheek I had received from relatives, or the cold, contractual press of the Duke's lips on my hand. This was a real kiss. And it was nothing, and everything, I had ever imagined.

It was not gentle. It was a collision. It was desperate and hungry, a release of all the yearning we had been forced to suppress for weeks. It was the taste of claret and longing. It was the feel of his hands, strong and sure, cupping my face as if I were something precious. I tasted the lie he had told me in the park, the pain of his rejection, and underneath it all, the burning, undeniable truth of his feelings.

My own hands, of their own volition, tangled in the soft, thick hair at the nape of his neck. I kissed him back with a ferocity that shocked me. I poured every ounce of my own hopeless love, my own lonely desperation, into that embrace. It was a confession. It was a surrender. In that moment, I was not Lady Araminta Wexley, the dutiful fiancée. I was just a woman, kissing the man she loved under the stars, damn the consequences.

He groaned, a low, guttural sound, and pulled me closer, his arm wrapping around my waist, molding my body to his. The world dissolved into a dizzying swirl of sensation. The scent of jasmine. The solid strength of him against me. The intoxicating taste of his mouth. It felt right. In a world of duty and cold arrangements, this one, profoundly wrong thing, felt more right than anything in my life.

When we finally, reluctantly, broke apart, we were both breathless, dizzy, our foreheads resting against each other. My eyes were closed. A slow, languid smile was spreading across my face. I felt incandescently happy.

I opened my eyes. And my world shattered.

He was standing not ten paces away, half-hidden in the deep shadows at the entrance to the arbor.

Thaddeus.

He was not in costume. He held his plain black mask in one hand, his knuckles white. His face was a pale, stark sculpture in the moonlight.

My heart did not just stop. It ceased to exist. The air in my lungs turned to ice. A scream, silent and sharp, clawed at the back of my throat. Every drop of blood in my body seemed to rush from my head, leaving me dizzy and sick with a terror so absolute it was paralyzing.

I stared at him, frozen in horror. The lingering warmth of Evander's kiss on my lips turned to ash. I expected an explosion. I expected a roar of ducal fury. I expected him to stride forward and strike his brother, to grab my arm and drag me from the garden in disgrace. I braced myself for the storm.

But the storm did not come.

He did not move. He did not speak. He did not scowl. His face was a blank, unreadable mask of perfect aristocratic control. He simply stood there, in the shadows, a silent witness to my utter and complete ruin.

His gaze, cold and grey as a winter sea, met mine. It held no anger. It held no pain. It held nothing at all. It was the gaze of a scientist observing an insect trapped in amber. It was the gaze of a judge looking upon a prisoner already condemned. The sheer, blank emptiness of it was more terrifying than any rage.

An eternity seemed to pass in that single, silent look. He saw everything. He saw my guilt. He saw the love I felt for his brother. He saw the ashes of his own honor at my feet.

And then, he did the most terrifying thing of all.

He broke eye contact. He gave a slow, almost imperceptible nod, as if acknowledging a truth he had long suspected. He turned, his movements precise and unhurried. And he walked away. He did not look back. He simply disappeared into the darkness of the gardens, swallowed by the night. He left behind a silence so profound, so heavy, it felt like a physical weight pressing down on me, crushing the very air from my lungs.

I was left trembling in the arbor, Evander's arms still loosely around me. The warmth of his body was no longer a comfort. It was a condemnation.

"Araminta?" Evander's voice was a choked whisper, his own face pale with shock.

But I could not answer. I could only stare at the empty space where the Duke had been. A shouting man is a predictable man. A furious man is a man you can reason with, a man whose anger will eventually burn itself out.

But a silent man? A man who witnesses the ultimate betrayal and walks away without a word? That is a man who is thinking. That is a man who is planning.

And in that moment, I knew with a certainty that chilled me to the bone, that the Duke's cold, quiet departure was not a reprieve. It was a verdict. And his silent, calculated fury would be a punishment far more terrible than any fleeting, passionate rage. The facade had not just been shattered. It had been annihilated. And I was left standing in the ruins, waiting for my sentence.

17

When the Masks Fall

Araminta

The silence in the arbor was a ringing in my ears. The spot where
Thaddeus had stood was a tear in the fabric of the night, a void that
pulsed with cold menace. He was gone. The world, which had stopped
for that one, perfect, ruinous kiss, now crashed back down upon me with the
weight of a collapsing building.

Panic, stark and absolute, seized me. It was a cold, sharp-clawed animal,
sinking its teeth into my heart. I had to find him. I had to explain. I had to
throw myself at his feet and beg his forgiveness. It was a fool's errand. An
impossible hope. But it was the only thing my mind, shattered into a thousand
pieces, could seize upon.

"Araminta?" Evander's voice was a choked whisper beside me. He reached
for my hand.

His touch was a lit torch against my skin. I recoiled as if burned.

"Don't!" The word was a strangled gasp, torn from my throat. I stumbled
back, away from him, my eyes wide with a horror that encompassed him,
myself, and the catastrophic thing we had just done. He was no longer the
charming man who had made me laugh. He was my accomplice. My ruin.

"Araminta, wait," he pleaded, taking a step toward me. "We must speak about this."

"There is nothing to speak about!" I cried, my voice a harsh, ugly sound. "You saw him. He knows. It is over."

My mind was a chaotic storm of recrimination. It was my fault. All of it. I had been weak. I had been selfish. I had indulged in a schoolgirl's fantasy and gambled with my family's entire future. And I had lost.

I turned and fled from the arbor. I ran, my silver gown snagging on thorns, my lungs burning. I did not look back to see if he followed. I did not care. He was the cause of this, and I was the cause, and I hated us both in that moment with a white-hot intensity.

I burst from the gardens back into the world of lanterns and music. The party was still in full swing. Masked figures laughed and drank, their faces joyous and carefree. They were living in a different world, one that had not just ended. I pushed through them, a desperate, wild-eyed ghost at their feast. My own gilded mask felt like a mockery, a cheap costume for a role I had just spectacularly failed to play.

Where would he have gone? The carriage? Would he leave without me? Without a word? The thought sent a fresh wave of ice through my veins.

I had to find him before he left.

I hurried into the main house, my soaked slippers making quiet, squelching sounds on the polished marble floors. The corridors were cooler here, and largely empty. The sound of the orchestra was a distant, mocking echo. I moved down a long, quiet hallway that led back toward the grand ballroom, my breath coming in ragged sobs.

And then I saw it.

It was lying in the middle of the floor, a stark black shape on the pale, checkered marble.

His mask.

He had discarded it. It lay there, abandoned, its empty eyeholes staring up at the ceiling. The sight was so final, so utterly symbolic, that it stopped me dead. The facade was gone. The pretense of the evening was over. He had shed the last vestige of social obligation and was now simply himself. The cold, silent Duke. The man I had betrayed.

I approached it slowly, as one might approach a fallen crown. I bent down, my fingers trembling, and picked it up. The black silk was cool and smooth in my hand. It held no warmth. It held no life. It was just a hollow thing. Like my future.

He was gone.

He had not waited. He had not sought a confrontation. He had simply vanished, leaving this one small token of his silent, terrifying fury.

The panic inside me collapsed, draining away to leave something far worse in its place. A cold, heavy, and absolute despair. There was nothing to be done. There was no one to plead with. I had played my hand, and the game was over.

Somehow, I found my way back to my mother. She was in the card room, absorbed in a game of whist, her face flushed with pleasure. She looked up as I approached, her smile faltering as she took in my appearance.

"Araminta, darling, you look pale as a sheet," she said, her voice a low murmur of concern. "Are you unwell?"

"A sudden headache, Mama," I whispered, the lie tasting like ash in my mouth. "I believe the heat has overcome me. Might we go home?"

The carriage ride was a silent torture. My mother chattered on about Lady Fitzroy's unfortunate choice of gown and the deliciousness of the salmon mousse. Her voice was a meaningless drone in the background of my own internal screaming. I sat rigid, staring out at the passing lights of London, the black silk mask clutched tightly in my lap. Every rotation of the carriage wheels felt like it was driving me further into my own personal hell.

When we finally reached our townhouse, I fled to my room. I did not wait for Eliza to help me with my gown. I tore at the buttons and laces myself, my fingers clumsy and shaking. The beautiful silver dress, the gown that had made me feel like a creature from a dream, now felt like the costume of a fool. It pooled on the floor, a shimmering puddle of my own disgrace.

I sank onto my bed, still in my chemise, and the dam of my composure finally broke. A single, wrenching sob escaped me, and then another, and another. The tears came in a hot, furious torrent, staining the silk of my pillow. It was a storm of grief, and fear, and a self-loathing so profound it felt like it would tear me apart.

I wept for the beautiful, foolish dream I had allowed myself to have. I wept for the man whose kiss had awakened my soul, only to condemn it. I wept for my own weakness, for my inability to be the dutiful, sensible daughter my family needed me to be.

My mind replayed the scene in the arbor. It was no longer romantic. It was a catastrophe viewed in stark, unforgiving detail. Evander's face, my own breathless response, our hands clinging to each other. And then, Thaddeus.

His silent form in the shadows was the image that burned brightest. His empty eyes. His controlled stillness. I had expected rage. I had been prepared for a shouting match, for public humiliation, for a dramatic severing of our engagement on the spot. I would have preferred it. An explosion of anger is a fire that eventually burns itself out.

But his silence... his silence was a cold, deep ocean. It promised not a quick, fiery end, but a slow, deliberate, and calculated drowning. A man who shouts has spent his anger. A man who is silent is a man who is thinking. He was planning my demise. And I had no doubt it would be a masterpiece of quiet, efficient cruelty.

What would he do? Would he simply send a note in the morning, a cold, formal dismissal that would set the tongues of the *ton* wagging for months? Would he tell my father, allowing the news to filter down and crush him with the weight of our renewed ruin? Or would he do something worse? Would he hold the threat over my family's head, using his power and my disgrace to extract some other price? The not-knowing was a form of madness.

And then, a new, more horrifying thought pierced through my selfish misery. This was not just about me. My actions had consequences that spread like ripples in a pond.

My father. I pictured his face, the hope that had returned to his eyes, the way he had begun to hold his head high again. This would destroy him. The debts would come crashing back down. The creditors would descend like vultures. He would be a broken man, and it would be my fault.

My mother. Her social ambitions, her life's work, would be annihilated. The Wexley name would be a joke, a cautionary tale whispered behind fans at every ball and soiree. She would be a social pariah.

My sisters. Elara and Phoebe. They were young and innocent. Their futures, their chances at good marriages, depended on the stability and reputation of our family. I had not just ruined my own prospects. I had poisoned theirs. Who would want to align their family with one tainted by such a public, humiliating scandal?

The weight of it all crushed me. My single, selfish act of desire, a few stolen moments of laughter and one reckless kiss, had doomed them all. The love I felt for Evander, which had seemed so bright and precious, now looked like a monstrous, selfish indulgence. The diamond ring on my dressing table was no longer a cage. It had been a lifeline. And I had severed it with my own two hands.

I buried my face in my pillow, my sobs quieting into a raw, hopeless ache. The masks were off. The game was over. I had gambled everything on a moment of passion, and now I, and everyone I loved, would have to pay the price. And I was terrified.

18

The Price of a Kiss

Evander

Guilt is a poison. It does not kill you outright. It seeps into your blood, slow and insidious, and corrodes you from the inside out. By the time I returned to Greycourt House, the poison was already working its black magic. My heart was a shriveled, aching thing in my chest.

The house was silent as a tomb. The servants had all retired. The gas lamps were turned low, casting long, skeletal shadows down the grand marble hallway. Every ticking clock, every creak of the floorboards, sounded like a judgment. I walked through the echoing silence, the ghost of Araminta's kiss still a phantom warmth on my lips, the image of my brother's face a brand on my mind.

I knew where he would be.

I went straight to his study. The door was closed. I did not knock. I had forfeited the right to such courtesies. I opened the door and stepped inside.

The room was empty. A single lamp burned on the massive mahogany desk, casting a pool of golden light on scattered parliamentary reports and neatly stacked correspondence. The room smelled of old leather, ink, and my brother's unwavering, suffocating sense of duty. It was the command center of his world, a world I had just set on fire.

I walked to the fireplace. I stood there, staring into the cold, dark grate, and I waited. The waiting was a torment. My mind was a relentless prosecutor, presenting its case with brutal clarity.

You knew she was engaged to your brother.

You pursued her.

You kissed her.

He saw you.

There was no defense. I was guilty on all counts. My charm, my wit, the easy excuses I had used my entire life to navigate the world, they were all useless now. They were the tools of a boy, and the crime I had committed was that of a man.

My gaze drifted to the portrait above the mantelpiece. It was our mother. She had been painted years ago, a beautiful, sad-eyed woman in a gown of pale blue. She looked out from the canvas with a gentle, melancholy expression, as if she knew the sorrows the world had in store for her sons. She had died at Northwood. The thought came unbidden, a splinter of ice in my heart.

I heard the sound of the door opening behind me. I did not have to turn. I felt the change in the room's atmosphere. The air grew colder, heavier. Thaddeus had arrived.

I turned slowly to face him. He stood by the door, his evening cloak still draped over his shoulders, his black mask held loosely in one hand. He looked as though he had just returned from a funeral. Perhaps he had. The funeral of his trust in me.

He closed the door with a soft, final click. He did not speak. He walked to his desk, his movements measured and precise. He placed the mask down on a stack of papers. He removed his gloves, finger by finger, and placed them beside the mask. The silence was absolute. It was a weapon, and he wielded it with surgical skill. He was making me wait. He was making me stew in the poison of my own guilt.

"Brother," I began, my voice a hoarse croak. I had to say something. I had to face the storm. "I..."

"There is nothing to say," he cut me off. His voice was not loud. It was quiet. It was perfectly, chillingly calm. It was the calm of a frozen lake, all the rage and fury locked away deep beneath the surface. He finally looked at me, and his grey eyes were like chips of flint. They held no fire. They held no warmth. They held nothing but a vast, empty coldness.

"Thaddeus, what you saw..."

"I saw exactly what I saw," he stated, his voice flat. He walked over to the decanter of brandy on a side table. He poured a single glass, his hand as steady as a rock. He did not offer one to me. "I saw my fiancée. And I saw my brother. In a moment of... indiscretion."

"It was my fault," I said quickly. Desperately. "Entirely my fault. Araminta is blameless. I pursued her. I pressed my suit when I should not have." I had to protect her. That was the only thing that mattered now. I had to take all the blame, all the fury, onto myself.

He took a slow sip of his brandy. He seemed to be considering my words. "Your fault," he repeated, his voice a low, thoughtful murmur. "Yes. I believe you are correct. It was your fault. You have always been governed by your appetites, Evander. By your whims. You have never understood the meaning of consequence." He set the glass down with a soft click. "You are about to learn."

I braced myself. For his anger. For his fists. For an order to get out of his house and never return.

What came was worse.

"You will leave London," he said, his voice still quiet, still controlled. "At dawn."

I nodded. It was what I had expected. A temporary banishment. An exile from society until the scandal, which was sure to erupt, died down. It was a fair price.

"I understand," I said.

"No," he replied, a flicker of something cold and sharp in his eyes. "I do not think you do." He paused, letting the silence stretch, letting the tension coil tighter and tighter in the room. "You will remove yourself to Northwood."

The name hit me like a physical blow. I felt the air leave my lungs. Northwood. The grey, windswept estate on the northern coast. The place of bleak skies and crashing waves. The place where our mother had withered away in a fog of melancholy. The place we had both avoided, by unspoken agreement, for more than a decade. It was not just a house. It was a tomb of our family's grief.

The cruelty of it was breathtaking. It was a punishment designed not just to remove me, but to wound me in the deepest, most personal way imaginable. This was not the act of a cold, dispassionate duke. This was the act of a brother whose betrayal had cut him to the bone, and who intended to return the favor with chilling precision.

"You will remain there," Thaddeus continued, his voice relentless, "until I summon you. Which may be some considerable time."

My throat was tight. I could not speak. I could only stare at him, at this man who was my brother, who was now my judge and my jailer. I saw the depth of his fury then, not in a shout, but in the cold, calculated cruelty of his command.

I had done this. My careless flirtation, my selfish desire, had led to this. I had hurt not only Araminta, but I had hurt my own brother so deeply that he would use our mother's memory as a weapon against me. The shame was a bitter, burning thing in my gut. I had earned this. Every bit of it.

"As you wish," I managed to say, my voice a broken whisper.

It was the only thing I could do. To argue, to protest, would only make things worse for her. My exile was the price of her protection. If I disappeared quietly, perhaps he would be merciful. Perhaps he would find a way to salvage the engagement, to protect her from the scandal I had created. It was a faint hope, but it was the only one I had.

He gave a single, sharp nod. The matter was closed. "See that you are gone by sunrise."

He turned his back on me then. He walked to his desk, sat down, and picked up a report as if I were no longer in the room. As if I had already ceased to exist. I was dismissed.

I stood there for a moment longer, a ghost in my brother's study. Then I turned and walked out, closing the door softly behind me.

I spent the next few hours in the lonely, pre-dawn silence of my own rooms. I instructed my valet to pack a single trunk. Necessities only. For a long stay.

Then, I sat at my desk. I took out a sheet of paper. I had to explain. I could not leave her with only the memory of my cruel words in the park. She deserved to know the truth.

My hand trembled as I wrote. The words poured out of me, a frantic, desperate confession.

```
My Dearest Araminta,
Forgive me. For everything. For my lies in the park. For my
weakness at the ball. For the ruin I have brought to your door.
The words I spoke to you at the gazebo were the greatest lie of my
life. You were never a game. You were never a diversion. From the
moment I met you, you have been a revelation. You have been the
only real thing in a world of pretense.
I am falling in love with you, Araminta. I think, perhaps, I
already have. And because I love you, I must leave you. I have
hurt you. I have hurt my brother. I have placed you in an
impossible, dangerous position. My presence can only cause you
more pain. My absence is the only gift I have left to give. It is
the only way I can protect you.
Do not think of me as a villain. Think of me as a fool who flew
too close to the sun and was burned. And who, in his foolishness,
scorched the one person he wished only to keep warm.
Be happy. Please. Find a way to be happy.
Yours, always,
Evander
```

I read the letter over, my vision blurring with unshed tears. The words were true. Every last one of them. And they were utterly, completely selfish.

What good would this letter do? It would not undo the damage. It would not save her from the consequences. It would only cause her more pain. It would burden her with the knowledge of my feelings, a knowledge that could only complicate her already impossible situation. It was not a gift. It was another claim on her heart, another weight she did not need to bear.

With a strangled cry of despair, I crushed the letter in my fist. The paper crumpled, my own words of love and regret turning to a worthless, wrinkled ball in my hand. It was my final act of love for her. Silence.

I threw the crumpled letter into the cold fireplace.

As the first, pale fingers of dawn stretched across the London sky, I walked out of Greycourt House. I did not look back. I was an exile, banished by my brother's cold fury. I was a man running from the wreckage of his own making. And my heart, which I had thought broken, felt as though it had been carved from my chest and left behind in that cold, silent house, along with a crumpled, unsent letter and the ghost of the woman I loved.

19

The Vanished Hopes

Araminta

I woke to a world made of grey. A dull, unforgiving light filtered through the heavy curtains of my bedroom window, illuminating dust motes dancing in the air like tiny, mocking ghosts. My head throbbed with a dull, persistent ache. It was the physical manifestation of a sleepless night spent wrestling with shame and terror.

I lay perfectly still under the weight of my bedclothes. I did not want to move. To move was to acknowledge the day had begun. And to begin the day was to begin waiting for the axe to fall. Every creak of the house, every distant shout from the street, sent a fresh jolt of adrenaline through me. I was a fox gone to ground, listening for the sound of the hunting horn.

Would it be a letter? A terse, formal note from the Duke's secretary, delivered on a silver tray, informing me that our arrangement was terminated. Or would he summon my father? I pictured Papa, his face pale and drawn, standing in that cold, imposing study at Greycourt House, listening as the Duke dismantled our family's future, piece by painful piece.

The silence was a living thing. It was a pressure against my eardrums, a weight on my chest. I had always thought of silence as an absence of sound. I now knew it was a presence. It was the sound of my own ruin, waiting in the

93

wings.

A soft knock at the door made me jump, my heart leaping into my throat.

"My lady?" Eliza's voice was quiet, hesitant.

"Come in," I managed to say, my own voice a dry, scratchy thing.

She entered, carrying a tray with a single cup of tea. Her eyes, shrewd and kind, took in my state in a single, sweeping glance. She saw the tangled sheets, the pallor of my skin, the dark, bruised-looking circles under my eyes. She did not comment. She simply set the tray down on my bedside table.

"A dreadful headache this morning, my lady?" she asked, her tone carefully neutral. She was offering me an excuse, a ready-made shield for my misery.

"Vicious," I confirmed, grateful for her tact. I pushed myself up against the pillows. The movement made my head swim. "The ball was... overwarm."

"Indeed, my lady." She moved to the window and drew back the heavy curtains. The grey morning light flooded the room, stark and unforgiving. I flinched. "Will you be receiving visitors today?"

The question was innocent. The implication was a sharp stab of fear. Would *he* be a visitor? Would the Duke arrive to deliver my sentence in person? The thought of facing him, of seeing that cold, empty gaze again, was so horrifying I felt a wave of nausea.

"No," I said quickly. "No visitors. I am not at home to anyone."

"Very good, my lady." She paused, her hands smoothing a wrinkle in the damask curtain. "There has been... no word? From Greycourt House?"

Her voice was soft, but the question was direct. She knew. Of course she knew something was deeply wrong. I had returned from the ball looking like a ghost, clutching a man's masquerade mask, and had wept for hours. Eliza was no fool.

"No," I said, my voice tight. "No word."

She said nothing more. She finished her tidying and left the room, leaving me alone with my tea and my terror. I did not touch the tea. The thought of swallowing anything was impossible.

The morning crawled by. Each tick of the mantel clock in the hallway was a drop of water torture. Ten o'clock. Eleven o'clock. Noon. Still nothing. The silence from Greycourt House was absolute. It was a deliberate, calculated weapon. He was not going to grant me the mercy of a swift end. He was going to let me dangle. He was going to let me marinate in my own shame and uncertainty.

By midday, I could bear it no longer. The not-knowing was a madness, a poison far more potent than my guilt. I had to do something. I had to know.

A desperate, foolish plan began to form in my mind.

I rang for Eliza. When she appeared, I was already out of bed, wrapped in my dressing gown.

"My writing things, please, Eliza," I said, my voice more forceful than it had been all morning. "And I will need one of the footmen to act as a messenger."

Her eyebrows rose a fraction of an inch, but she did not question me. She brought me my small, portable writing desk, with its neat stack of paper, its inkwell, and its pens.

I sat down, my hands trembling. What was I doing? This was a terrible idea. To reach out, to break the silence myself, was a sign of weakness. It was to show him how deeply his silence affected me. But I no longer cared about strategy. I cared only about ending this excruciating limbo.

My pen hovered over the paper. I could not ask about Evander. It would be a confession in itself. My inquiry had to be directed at the Duke. It had to be a perfect performance of wifely concern.

My dearest Duke, I began, then immediately scratched it out. Too familiar. Too intimate.

Your Grace, I wrote, my script a little shaky.

```
I trust you are well after the exertions of last evening. I
confess the heat of the ball left me with a formidable headache,
from which I am only just recovering. I hope you did not suffer
any similar ill effects.
```

It was a masterpiece of vapid, meaningless prose. It said nothing. It asked for nothing. But it was a line cast into the silent, deep waters of his displeasure. I was fishing for a response. Any response at all.

I folded the note. I sealed it with my plainest wax. The real reason for my inquiry was a shameful, frantic pulse beneath the surface of the polite words.

I did not truly care about the Duke's health. I was desperate for news of his brother. Had he been thrown out? Had they fought? Was he still in London? The note was a pretense, a key forged to unlock a door I was terrified to open.

I gave the letter to a young footman named Thomas, my instructions clipped and precise. "To Greycourt House. For His Grace, the Duke of Renshawe. Wait for a reply."

And then, I waited.

The hour that followed was the longest of my life. I paced my room. I stared out the window. I rearranged the books on my shelf. I did anything to keep from screaming. My hope was a fragile, pathetic thing. Perhaps Evander would fight for me. Perhaps the kiss had meant enough that he would confront his brother, that he would refuse to let me go. Perhaps Thaddeus, seeing the depth of our feelings, would be moved to some form of mercy, some quiet dissolution of the engagement that would spare us all public ruin.

They were the foolish, desperate hopes of a condemned woman praying for a last-minute pardon.

Thomas returned.

I heard his footsteps in the hall. I flew to the door, my heart pounding a frantic, breathless rhythm. He stood there, holding not a letter, but a small, stiff calling card.

He handed it to me. It was from the Duke's secretary, a man named Mr. Abernathy, whose name was as dry and dusty as he was.

On the back, a few lines were scrawled in a neat, impersonal script.

```
His Grace is in good health and appreciates your inquiry.
```

That was it. My polite question had been met with an equally polite, and utterly dismissive, reply. But there was more. Another line, added as if it were an afterthought of no importance whatsoever.

```
Lord Evander departed London this morning on urgent family
business.
```

The card fell from my fingers. It fluttered to the carpet, a small white flag of my own surrender.

Gone.

He was gone.

He had not fought for me. He had not sent me a word. He had not stayed to face the consequences beside me. He had simply... left. The man who had kissed me with such desperate passion in the moonlight had vanished with the morning mist. My foolish hope that our connection meant something more than a reckless flirtation shattered into a million tiny, sharp pieces. His words in the park had not been a lie to protect me. They had been the simple, brutal truth. I had been a game, and when the game became dangerous, he had simply walked away from the board.

And the lie. *Urgent family business.* It was so transparent, so chillingly efficient. This was not a flight. This was an exile. Thaddeus, in his cold, silent fury, had banished his own brother. He had dealt with one half of the problem swiftly and ruthlessly.

And now, only I remained.

The silence from the Duke was no longer a mystery. It was a strategy. He was isolating me. He had removed the man I loved from the equation. Now, I was alone, at his mercy. The limbo was not a sign of his indecision. It was a cage, and he was slowly, deliberately, locking the door.

My knees felt weak. I stumbled back to a chair, sinking into it. The last vestiges of my hope drained away, leaving a cold, hollow emptiness.

I had lost them both.

One had abandoned me. The other was now my tormentor, my fate held in his cold, silent hands. The future, which had once been a solid, if unhappy, certainty, was now a terrifying blank. The security of the engagement was gone. The dream of a life with Evander was a pathetic, childish fantasy.

I was left with nothing. Nothing but the crushing weight of my own foolish, selfish actions. My once-secure future was now hanging by a single, fraying thread, and the man holding the shears was the Duke of Renshawe. And he, I knew with a certainty that chilled me to my very soul, was in no hurry to let it drop.

20

The Rumors and Regrets

Araminta

T he days that followed were a masterclass in psychological torture. A week passed. The silence from Greycourt House was a living entity, a suffocating blanket that smothered all hope. Evander had vanished from London. The Duke had vanished from my life. And I was left to drift in the terrifying, uncertain space between betrothed and disgraced.

My mother, however, was a warrior. Her battlefield was the drawing rooms of London, and her weapon was a relentless, unshakeable denial. To her, the problem was not the gaping wound in our family's prospects, but the perception of it. If we carried on as normal, she reasoned, then everything *was* normal. Hiding away was an admission of guilt. And so, I was to be paraded about as proof of our continued social solvency.

"The Ladies' Auxiliary Committee luncheon," she announced one morning, her voice bright with a terrifying cheerfulness. "For the new charity hospital. We must attend. It is our duty. And Lady Danbury will be expecting us."

"Mama, I am not well," I protested, the excuse sounding weak even to my own ears.

"Nonsense," she declared, her eyes sharp. "You will put on your new jonquil silk, you will smile, and you will show the world that the future Duchess of

Renshawe is in excellent spirits. We will give them nothing to talk about."

She did not understand. They already had something to talk about. We were simply arriving to provide a visual aid for their gossip.

The luncheon was held at the London home of the Countess of Abernathy. The air in the countess's drawing room was thick with the scent of hothouse lilies and hypocrisy. It was a sea of pastel silks, nodding feathered hats, and sharp, predatory eyes. I felt like a Christian being led into the Colosseum, my smile a pathetic shield against the hungry lions of the *ton*.

I took a cup of tea, my hand trembling slightly. I could feel the stares. They were not overt, but I felt them all the same. The quick, assessing glance that flickered away the moment I looked up. The sudden hush in a conversation as I drew near. It was the social equivalent of being dissected by a thousand tiny, invisible knives. My paranoia was a fever, and every polite smile I received was a fresh wave of heat.

"Lady Araminta, how lovely to see you out." It was Lady Cowper, a woman whose face was a permanent mask of pleased condescension. "We had heard you were... indisposed."

The word hung in the air, weighted with unspoken meaning.

"A slight headache merely," I replied, my own voice a cool, distant echo. "The summer heat has been most trying."

"Indeed," she said, her eyes glittering. "It can lead one to do the most... impulsive things."

She smiled, a thin, knowing curve of her lips, and moved away to greet someone else, leaving me with the distinct feeling that I had just been elegantly insulted.

I tried to lose myself in a corner. I found a seat near a potted fern and pretended to be fascinated by the pattern on my teacup. But I could not escape the whispers. The room was a murmuring hive of speculation, and I was the unfortunate flower at its center.

I needed to escape. On the pretense of seeking a second biscuit, I stood and made my way toward the refreshment table. It required me to pass by a small settee where two women sat in quiet, intense conversation. One was a Miss Albright, a notorious gossip with a face like a perpetually startled pekinese. The other was the formidable Lady Satterthwaite, a woman whose pronouncements could make or break a debutante's entire season.

I tried to glide past them unnoticed. But their voices, though low, were sharp and clear.

"... a disgraceful scene, from what I hear," Miss Albright was saying, her voice a conspiratorial hiss. "In the gardens at Vauxhall. Quite thrown himself at her, apparently."

My blood turned to ice. I froze, my back to them, pretending to examine a plate of lemon tarts.

"And with the Duke's own brother!" Lady Satterthwaite replied, her voice a low rumble of disapproval. "It is beyond the pale. The lack of decorum is simply staggering. Thaddeus Greycourt is not a man to be made a fool of."

"Indeed not," Miss Albright agreed with relish. "I imagine the engagement will be broken any day now. It is only a matter of time before the announcement is made. Such a shame. The Wexley girl was set to make such an advantageous match."

"She has no one to blame but herself," Lady Satterthwaite pronounced with grim finality. "A moment of foolishness can ruin a lifetime of prospects."

I could not breathe. The air in my lungs had solidified. My private, secret shame was now a commodity, a piece of juicy gossip being traded over tea and cakes. It was real. It was out. And it was spreading like a plague.

My cheeks burned with a heat so intense I felt dizzy. I turned, my movements stiff and jerky, and fled the room. I did not stop until I reached the cool, empty quiet of the entrance hall. I leaned against a marble pillar, my hand pressed to my churning stomach, and fought against the wave of nausea that threatened to overwhelm me.

The polite smiles of the other ladies were daggers of judgment. Every kind inquiry was a veiled accusation. The weight of my regret, of my fear, became a physical presence, a crushing weight on my chest that made it impossible to draw a full breath.

The journey home was a silent, agonizing blur. My mother knew something had happened. She kept casting worried, questioning glances at me, but for once, she did not press. I think she was afraid of the answer.

When we arrived at our townhouse, I went straight to my father's study. I do not know why. Perhaps I simply needed to see him, to confess, to throw myself on his mercy.

I found him sitting behind his large desk. He was not reading. He was staring at a single sheet of paper in his hand. His face was the color of ash. His shoulders were slumped in a way I had not seen since the dark days before my engagement, the days when the creditors were at our door.

He looked up as I entered. His eyes were full of a hollow, defeated sadness.

"Papa?" I whispered, my heart clenching with a new, fresh dread. "What is it?"

He did not have to answer. I knew. I knew from the expensive paper. I knew from the stark, black ink. I knew from the look on his face.

"A letter," he said, his voice a hoarse croak. "From the Duke."

He held it out to me. My hand trembled as I took it. The letter was brutally, chillingly brief.

```
Lord Wexley,
Due to unforeseen circumstances, I find it necessary to postpone
the wedding between myself and your daughter, Lady Araminta.
The postponement is indefinite.
I remain your servant,
Renshawe
Indefinite.
```

The word was a death sentence. It was not a severing. It was not a clean break. An engagement broken, while scandalous, is at least final. But a postponement, an indefinite one, was a public declaration of uncertainty. It was a masterpiece of social warfare. It did not release me. It trapped me. It hung me in a state of public limbo, my name and my family's honor left to twist in the winds of gossip and speculation. Everyone would know something was wrong. Everyone would whisper. Everyone would wonder. He was not ending the scandal. He was feeding it.

The walls of the study seemed to close in on me. I felt a wave of dizziness, a sense of being trapped, suffocated.

My private mistake was now a public spectacle. The Duke was not going to release me with a quiet, merciful cut. He was going to let me bleed out, slowly, publicly, where everyone could watch.

My father's heartbroken gaze met mine. My mother's desperate social climbing, my sisters' futures, it all swirled in the suffocating air around me.

And in that moment, I realized the truth. My greatest fear should not have been a confrontation with the Duke. It should not have been his anger. My greatest fear should have been his silence. Because his silence was a cage.

And I was now locked inside it. The weight of regret was no longer just a feeling. It was a physical reality, a prison of his making. And I saw, with a terrible, stark clarity, that sitting here, doing nothing, waiting for his next move, was no longer just a passive suffering. It was a choice. It was a choice to let him destroy us.

And a new feeling began to stir in the ashes of my despair. It was not hope. It was something harder. Sharper. It was the dawning, terrifying realization that my only path to salvation did not lie in waiting for mercy. It lay in escape.

21

Run or Ruin

Araminta

The letter lay on my father's desk. A single sheet of paper. A graveyard for my family's hopes. The word *indefinite* was not an ink blot. It was a brand. It marked me. It marked us all. I stood there, frozen in the dusty, book-scented air of the study, and felt the four walls of my life contract until they were the size of a coffin.

My father's head was still bowed. He looked up at me, his eyes hollowed out by a grief so profound it seemed to have aged him a decade in a single afternoon. He saw the letter still in my hand. He saw the understanding dawning in my eyes. He did not have to speak. We were united in our silent comprehension of the catastrophe.

The door to the study burst open. My mother stood on the threshold. She had clearly just returned from her own social rounds, her face a mask of furious, terrified energy. She held a calling card in her gloved hand as if it were a venomous snake she had just killed.

"I have just come from Lady Grantham's," she announced, her voice a low, trembling wire of rage. "She offered me her pity, Eustace. Her pity! She asked if there was any truth to the unfortunate rumors surrounding Araminta's engagement." She advanced into the room, her gaze sweeping from my father's defeated form to my own pale face. "What has happened? What does that letter say?"

My father could not answer. He seemed to have shrunk into his chair. I held the Duke's letter out to her. My hand was surprisingly steady. There is a strange calm that comes when the worst has already happened.

She snatched it from me. Her eyes flew across the brutally brief lines. I watched the last vestiges of color drain from her face. Her carefully constructed composure, the armor she wore to face the world, shattered. Her mouth opened, but no sound came out. Then, she crumpled the letter in her fist, her knuckles white.

"No," she whispered. Then, louder, her voice cracking with disbelief and fury. "No! He cannot do this. We had an agreement. A contract."

"It would seem he can, Beatrice," my father said, his voice a weary rasp.

She spun on him. "And you will just sit there? You will let him ruin us? After everything? After the sacrifice *she* has made?" She pointed a trembling finger at me.

"What would you have me do?" he asked, his voice raw with despair. "Challenge a duke to a duel? He holds all the cards. He always has."

"Then *she* must do something!" My mother turned her wild, panicked eyes on me. "This is your fault, Araminta. Your foolish, selfish behavior! The rumors, Araminta! Do you have any idea what they are whispering about you because of your thoughtless actions? Did you think there would be no consequences? You must go to him. You must go to the Duke and you must beg his forgiveness."

The words were so absurd, so utterly disconnected from the reality of the man I was engaged to, that I almost laughed. The sound that escaped me was a dry, broken thing. "Beg?" I repeated. "Mama, you do not understand him. Thaddeus does not respond to begging. He responds to logic. To leverage. And I have none."

"Then find some!" she shrieked, taking a step toward me. Her face was a twisted mask of fear. "You will go to that house, and you will get on your knees if you must. You will weep. You will tell him you were a fool. You will tell him you love him. You will tell him whatever lies are necessary to fix what you have broken. You will save this family. Do you understand me?"

The thought of kneeling before Thaddeus, of performing some pathetic, groveling display of false contrition, was so revolting it made my stomach turn. He would not be moved. He would only watch me, his eyes cold and empty, enjoying my humiliation. He would savor the proof of his power over me. It would grant me nothing. It would only cost me the last shred of my dignity.

"No," I said, my voice quiet but firm. "I will not."

"You will not?" My mother's voice rose to a shrill peak. "You selfish, ungrateful girl! After everything we have done for you, everything we have given you, you will not even try to save us from the ruin you have brought down upon our heads? Your sisters, Araminta! Have you thought of them? Have you thought of Elara and Phoebe? Their prospects will be dust. They will be tainted by your scandal. We will all be outcasts, all because you could not control yourself for one evening in a garden!"

Each word was a lash. Each accusation was true, in its own way. The weight of it pressed down on me, and I felt myself begin to crumble. The tears I had held back for so long burned behind my eyes.

"Beatrice, that is enough."

It was my father's voice. He had risen from his chair. He came to my side, a frail but determined shield. He put a hand on my arm.

"She is wrong, Eustace," my mother sobbed, her fury collapsing into ragged despair. "She has destroyed us all."

"No," he said, his voice trembling with a sorrow that was far more painful than my mother's rage. He looked at me, his eyes full of a deep, heartbreaking contrition. "I destroyed us. I did this. I did this the moment I signed away my daughter's happiness to pay for my own foolish mistakes."

He turned to me, his hand tightening on my arm. His face was pale. His eyes were wet. "Araminta, my dear girl," he said, his voice thick with unshed tears. "Look at me. If you cannot go through with this marriage... if you cannot bear it... I will understand. We will face the consequences. Together. I will not have you sacrifice one more moment of your life for my errors. Your happiness is worth more than this house, more than our name, more than anything."

His absolution was a kindness so profound it broke my heart. It was a release I did not deserve. And it was an impossible choice.

I stood there, trapped between them. My mother's condemnation and my father's forgiveness. One demanded I sacrifice my dignity to save our future. The other offered to sacrifice our future to save my dignity. One path led to a groveling, soul-crushing performance before a man who despised me. The other led to a noble, shared poverty, watching my family pay the price for my actions every single day.

Both were unbearable. Both paths led to a prison.

And in that moment of perfect, agonizing clarity, as my mother wept and my father offered a forgiveness that would ruin him, I saw a third path.

It was not a path to happiness. It was not a path to redemption. It was a narrow, dangerous track through the wilderness, a path I would have to cut myself. But it was a path of my own making.

I gently removed my father's hand from my arm. I looked from his grief-stricken face to my mother's terrified one. They were trapped in this disaster with me. As long as I was here, in London, a subject of gossip, a pawn in the Duke's cruel game, they would be trapped. My presence was the anchor that was dragging us all down.

The decision solidified in my mind. It was not a flash of inspiration. It was a cold, hard, and inevitable piece of logic. If I could not fix what I had broken, I could at least remove the broken pieces from the board.

"Please," I said, my voice surprisingly calm and steady. "Both of you. Please stop."

I walked out of the study, leaving them in a stunned, unhappy silence. I went up to my room. I closed the door. I did not weep. The time for tears was over. The time for action had begun.

To run would require money. Not a great deal, but enough. Enough to buy a ticket on a mail coach. Enough to secure a room in a boarding house in some forgotten town where no one knew my name.

My eyes scanned the room. I had nothing of real value. My jewelry was mostly costume, pretty baubles of little worth. Except for one piece.

I went to my jewelry box. I opened a small, satin-lined drawer at the bottom.

There it lay. A necklace of perfectly matched pearls, clasped with a small diamond. It had been my grandmother's. She had given it to me on my sixteenth birthday. It was my most cherished possession. It was the only thing of true value that was mine and mine alone.

The thought of selling it was a physical pain, a sharp grief for the girl I had once been. But that girl was gone. And sentiment was a luxury I could no longer afford.

But how? I could not simply walk into a jeweler's shop on Bond Street. A lady of my station selling her pearls would be a fresh scandal before the day was out.

Eliza.

I rang the bell. When she appeared, I was calm. My resolve had hardened into something cold and unshakeable.

"Eliza," I said, my voice low and even. "I require your help. And your absolute discretion. Can I trust you?"

She looked at my face, at the necklace in my hand. Her own face was pale, but her eyes were steady. She had served my family since she was a girl. She had seen me through scraped knees and childish heartbreaks. She saw the truth now.

"Always, my lady," she whispered.

I held out the necklace. "I need you to sell this for me. Not in our neighborhood. Somewhere far from here. A pawn shop. A money-lender. I do not care. I do not care what price you get. I just need the money. As much as you can get. And no one can ever know."

She took the pearls from my hand. Her fingers trembled slightly as they closed around them. She understood the magnitude of what I was asking. This was not just a transaction. This was a severing. This was the funding of an escape.

"It will be done, my lady," she said, her voice firm. She slipped the necklace into the pocket of her apron. "Tomorrow. I will find a way."

She curtseyed and left, leaving me alone in the quiet room.

I stood by the window, looking out at the city that had been my home, my playground, and now my prison. The decision was made. The die was cast.

This was not an act of passion. It was a calculated retreat. I was not running to something. I was not running to find Evander. He was a ghost, a dream that had cost me everything.

I was running from ruin. By leaving, I might spare Thaddeus the continued humiliation of our public, broken engagement. I could remove myself as a weapon he could use against my family. My disappearance would cause a brief, sharp scandal, but it would be a final one. It would cauterize the wound.

It was a painful, terrifying choice, born of guilt and a desperate, primal yearning to be free. But it was my choice. The first real choice I had made since this whole nightmare began.

The stage was set. Tomorrow, my last tie to my old life would be cut. And then, I would run. And I prayed it would be enough to save what was left of us all.

22

Flight Before Dawn

Araminta

T he hours before dawn are a dead time. A quiet, breathless pause in the life of a great city. London slept. But I did not. I sat on the edge of my bed, fully dressed, a stranger in my own room. I wore my plainest, darkest traveling dress. It was a serviceable grey wool, the kind of dress a governess or a poor relation might wear. It was my new skin. My valise, small and pitifully light, sat by the door. It contained two changes of clothes, a book of poetry I could not bear to leave behind, and my dwindling courage.

The house was silent. It was a deep, unsettling quiet, filled with the ghosts of sleeping people. My family. I imagined them in their beds, unaware of the betrayal I was about to commit. Or was it a salvation? I no longer knew. My heart hammered against my ribs, a frantic, trapped bird. Every creak of the floorboards in the hallway, every distant rattle of a cart on a faraway street, sounded like the approach of doom.

A soft scratch at my door made me jump, my hand flying to my mouth to stifle a gasp.

The door opened a sliver. Eliza slipped inside, a shadow in the darkness. She was also dressed, a heavy cloak covering her servant's uniform. She held a small, heavy purse in her hand.

"It is done, my lady," she whispered, her voice a low, urgent breath. She pressed the purse into my hand. The coins inside clinked with a soft, final sound. It was the ghost of my grandmother's pearls. "And the ticket. For the northbound mail coach. It leaves from a coaching inn near Cheapside in less than an hour."

"Thank you, Eliza," I breathed, my voice thick with an emotion I could not name. Gratitude. Fear. Sorrow. "I will never forget this."

"Nor I, my lady." Her eyes, even in the dim light, were shining with tears. "Be safe. Be clever." She squeezed my hand, a quick, desperate pressure. "Godspeed."

She slipped back out of the room as silently as she had entered, a loyal, steadfast ghost.

Now, only one task remained. The final severing.

I moved to my writing desk. The two sheets of paper lay waiting, stark and white in the moonlight. I picked up my pen. My hand was shaking so violently I could barely form the letters.

The first letter was the hardest. *My dearest Mama and Papa.* The words were a knife in my own heart. I wrote of my love. I wrote of my profound, bottomless regret for the pain I was about to cause them. I did not explain the details of my ruin. They knew enough. I wrote only that I could not, in good conscience, drag them further into the disaster I had created. My departure, I explained, was not an act of rebellion, but an act of protection. It was a lie, and it was the truth. I prayed that one day, they might understand. And forgive me.

The second letter was easier. It was colder. It was an execution.

My script was firm, my hand steady now. There was no emotion in the words. There was only business. A contract being terminated.

```
Your Grace,
I write to inform you that I can no longer proceed with our
arrangement. Please consider our engagement, and any and all
obligations between our two families, formally and irrevocably
dissolved.
I wish you a good life.
```

Araminta Wexley

I did not sign it as his future duchess. I did not even sign it as 'sincerely' or 'yours'. I was simply Araminta Wexley. A name he could now erase from his ledgers.

I folded each letter. I sealed them with plain, anonymous wax. There was no turning back now. The words were written. The deeds were done.

It was time.

I picked up my valise. I took one last look around the room that had been my entire world. The pretty wallpaper. The familiar furniture. The ghosts of my childhood. I closed the door on all of it, a soft, final click in the sleeping house.

Every step down the grand staircase was a fresh wave of terror. The third step from the top had always creaked. I held my breath, stepping over it. The air was cold and still. The moonlight streamed through the tall windows in the entrance hall, painting the checkered marble floor in eerie squares of black and white. It felt like a chessboard. And I was a pawn making a desperate, unauthorized move across the board.

I placed the two letters on the polished hall table, side by side. They looked small and momentous in the vast, silent space.

My hand was on the heavy brass handle of the front door when I heard it. A soft sound from above. A cough. My blood turned to ice. My father. Was he awake? Was he coming down? I froze, my body rigid, every muscle screaming. I waited, not breathing, for what felt like an eternity.

Silence.

I did not wait another second. I turned the handle. The mechanism was loud in the stillness, a series of clicks that sounded like gunshots to my terrified ears. I pulled the heavy door open just enough to slip through.

And then I was outside.

The city air was cool and damp. A fine, misty drizzle was falling, slicking the cobblestones until they gleamed like polished slate in the faint glow of the gas lamps. The world was quiet, hushed, waiting for the dawn.

I pulled the hood of my dark cloak over my head and began to walk. I did not run. To run was to draw attention. I walked with a steady, determined pace, my valise bumping against my leg. My heart was a wild, frantic thing, pounding out a rhythm of fear and adrenaline. Every shadow was a threat. Every distant noise was the sound of discovery. A nosy neighbor peering from a window. A watchman on his rounds. I kept my head down, my eyes fixed on the wet, dark ground before me.

The journey to the coaching inn was a blur of dark alleyways and sleeping streets. The London I knew, a city of bright carriages and crowded shops, was gone. This was its secret, nighttime self, a place of shadows and secrets. A fitting place for my escape.

I saw it at the end of a narrow, dirty street. The mail coach. It was a lumbering, dark beast of a thing, its lamps casting a weak, yellow glow in the gloom. Horses stamped and snorted, their breath pluming in the damp air. A few other shadowy figures, cloaked and silent like myself, were already boarding.

This was it. The vessel of my escape.

My ticket, secured by Eliza's courage and my grandmother's pearls, was a crumpled piece of paper in my fist. I handed it to the grim-faced coachman. He grunted and gestured me inside.

I climbed the steep steps, my legs trembling. The interior of the coach was dark and cramped. It smelled of damp wool, old leather, and the faint, sour smell of strangers. I found a seat by the window and shrank into the corner, pulling my cloak tightly around me as if it could make me invisible.

The door slammed shut, a sound of absolute finality. With a lurch and a groan of protesting wood, the coach began to move.

It rumbled over the cobblestones, away from the inn, away from the familiar streets, away from my entire life. We passed through the sleeping city, a ghost ship sailing through a ghost town.

As we crossed a bridge over the Thames, the first, faint rays of dawn began to break over the horizon. The sky to the east was a pale, bruised purple, streaked with a fragile, hopeful pink. The rising sun caught the spires and rooftops of London, turning the city into a dark, jagged silhouette against the growing light.

I stared out the coach window, my hand pressed against the cold glass. And the tears I had held back for so long finally came. They were not the hot, furious tears of grief from the night before. They were cold, silent tears of mourning.

I mourned the family I was leaving behind. I mourned the girl I had been, the one whose future had been so certain. I mourned the love I had found and lost, the ghost of Evander's smile, the memory of his arms around me.

But underneath the terror, underneath the profound, soul-deep sorrow, a new feeling stirred. It was a strange, terrifying, and unfamiliar sensation.

It was freedom.

The chains were broken. The contract was void. The Duke's cold, silent power over me was gone. My life was no longer a predetermined path. It was a blank, unmarked map, and I was heading into the wilderness with no guide.

I, Araminta Wexley, was terrified. I was heartbroken. And I was, for the first time, entirely, breathtakingly, on my own.

The coach picked up speed, leaving the last vestiges of the city behind. I did not look away from the window until the familiar skyline had completely disappeared. There was nothing ahead but the open road and the uncertain dawn. And I had no idea what came next.

* * *

Thank you for spending time with Lady Araminta Wexley and her thoroughly inconvenient engagement.

If you gasped, grinned, or considered eloping with a charming younger brother of your own—then my work here is delightfully done.

But of course, one stolen kiss rarely ends a story.

And Araminta's has only just begun.

Stay tuned for the next installment:

How to Break the Rules and Marry His Brother

Coming soon, with even more scandal, mischief, and one very confused duke.

With all my thanks and a conspiratorial wink ^^

Cressida Blythewood

23

Thank You

Hello, dearest sweetheart

This little book is what I like to call a bite-sized romance: short, swoony, and perfectly suited for a cozy evening with tea (or wine— we don't judge).

It's a novella, which means you can read it in one delicious sitting—ideal for when you crave just enough scandal, stolen glances, and emotional chaos to make your heart flutter without committing to a 400-page affair.

I've always adored full-length novels, but with this one, I wanted to try something a little different—a novella that still feels rich, romantic, and just the right amount of reckless.

Expect banter, heartbreak, and one wildly inconvenient duke... all wrapped up in a story that doesn't overstay its welcome.

I hope it leaves you smiling, sighing, and maybe just a little bit desperate for the next one.

With love (and a wink),

Cressida Blythewood

Printed in Dunstable, United Kingdom

70775301R00070